Say it, Scarlett. *"We messed it up, before. And it wasn't fun. The contrast between the—between what we had in bed, and the rest—"*

He answered slowly, "We were different people, then. In a different situation."

"Different enough, compared with the people we are now?"

"That weekend…" He leaned closer, looked down at their joined hands, rubbed the pad of his thumb over her knuckles in slow strokes.

"Yes, can we talk about that weekend?" she said. "We need to."

How? She sensed it wasn't going to be easy. The noise level in the beer garden was rising. Hard to tell if the other conversations going on would be a protection or would force them to talk uncomfortably loud.

She stretched forward, almost knocking down her beer, so that their heads were close. Listening distance. Debating distance. Kissing distance, almost.

Almost, but not quite.

Dear Reader,

Several times a year, I drive a particular Australian road which takes me past a massive sprawl of old cars, many of which have been there for more than fifty years. They are now valuable for their rare spare parts, and have become a local tourist attraction. You can see this place and read about it for yourself if you search the internet for "Flynn's Wreckers Cooma." When I started writing Scarlett and Daniel's story, I had no idea that a car yard similar to this one—smaller, though—was going to be important in the story, but it soon emerged as a significant part of Daniel's past. With Scarlett's help, he will need to work through his history and deal with the legacy of those cars before they have a hope of building a future together.

This is one of the things I love about writing. Something that starts off as a small detail can take on a major and meaningful role, and you have to wonder if my subconscious knew better than I did, and had been storing up my impressions of Flynn's wrecking yard all these years.

Scarlett and Daniel had a sizzling encounter several years before this story starts, but it was a classic case of meeting at the wrong time. Now that they've found each other again, they soon discover that the same things that broke them apart before could shatter everything a second time. I hope you enjoy their journey.

Lilian Darcy

A DOCTOR
IN HIS HOUSE

LILIAN DARCY

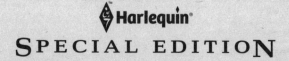

Harlequin®

SPECIAL EDITION

Recycling programs
for this product may
not exist in your area.

ISBN-13: 978-0-373-65668-4

A DOCTOR IN HIS HOUSE

Books by Lilian Darcy

LILIAN DARCY

has written nearly eighty books for Silhouette Romance, Special Edition and Harlequin Medical Romance (Prescription Romance). Happily married, with four active children and a very patient cat, she enjoys keeping busy and could probably fill several more lifetimes with the things she likes to do—including cooking, gardening, quilting, drawing and traveling. She currently lives in Australia but travels to the United States as often as possible to visit family. Lilian loves to hear from readers. You can write to her at P.O. Box 532, Jamison P.O., Macquarie ACT 2614, Australia, or email her at lilian@liliandarcy.com.

Chapter One

It began with a familiar headache, which grew steadily worse as Scarlett drove north to Vermont. She pulled over, swallowed painkillers and kept driving, but ten miles from her brother's house, before the painkillers could kick in, her vision began to blur as if her eyes were windowpanes and there was water running down the glass.

She almost stopped driving at that point, but by the time she'd found a place to pull over, the water seemed to have stopped running and she could see clearly again. Things didn't feel quite right. On top of the pain, her brain felt foggy and disconnected. But she was less than ten minutes from Andy's, so it seemed best to keep on going. After all, she'd had these spells before.

The symptoms had been milder those other times, though. Self-diagnosis followed by several tests to rule out more serious options had settled on migraine. The spells always passed before they cost her any significant time at work.

And before they forced her to question the way she was living her life.

Today, the real trouble hit two miles from her destination, and this time there was no warning. The whole world just keeled over like a ship run aground, except she knew the problem wasn't with the world, it was inside her head. Even though she was wearing chunky sunglasses with dark lenses, the daylight felt so bright that it blinded her, and her senses were scrambled and out of her control.

No question about waiting for a safe place to pull over now.

The safe place had to be right here, because another five seconds at the wheel and she would crash. She couldn't see, could barely move… She just managed to brake hard, bring the car to a halt and kill the engine, a couple of hundred yards from the Radford town boundary, and she could only hope she was on the shoulder not the road.

Then she rolled the window down and sat.

Fought the dizziness and pain.

Waited, with her hands gripping the top of the steering wheel and her forehead pressed hard against it, for the moment when she would feel well enough to leave the car, or find the phone that lay in her purse.

But the moment didn't happen. If she tried to open her eyes, all she saw was painful, blinding brightness. If she moved an inch, the world tilted and rolled. She groped for her purse, but it was out of reach on the floor of the passenger seat where it must have slid when she'd braked so suddenly.

She lost track of time, although it must have been fifteen minutes or more. It felt like forever, a terrifying, featureless landscape of unraveling minutes in which all she could do was to stay motionless, keep breathing and think about what had brought her to this point. Andy had been right in his older-brother concern about her stress levels and working hours, and his insistence that she listened to Dad too much. This trip to Vermont was meant to signal a shift in her priorities, but her body was telling her that it had come too late.

Cars went past. She heard the *whoosh* of the air and the hum of their engines. No one slowed or stopped. Maybe they thought she was taking a phone call or checking an address. The painkillers she'd taken earlier began to work and the dizziness eased a little. She thought again about trying to reach for the purse.

But before she could make the move, she heard the sound of tires popping on gravel, the rumble and surge of an automatic transmission shifting gears and the slam of a car door.

Even her hearing had gone haywire, because she couldn't tell which direction any of it was coming from. Behind her? Far side of the road? She didn't know whether to call out or stay silent.

She heard footsteps crunching on the gravel shoulder. They stopped beside her open car window. A man cleared his throat. "Everything okay here, ma'am?" The voice was gravelly and slow and faintly threatening. Again, she didn't know what to do. Wish it would go away, or ask it for help?

"Um, yes, just resting my eyes," she lied, to buy a little time. Maybe in a few seconds she could summon the ability to open her eyes and move enough to look at him, see what kind of a man he was, whether he looked as if she could trust him.

She tried it, letting a slit of vision appear between her lids, but the light and blurring hit with merciless speed and she couldn't see a thing.

There was a pause. The voice stayed silent, but the feet

didn't move. Then the man spoke again, deliberate and slow. "I'm a Vermont state trooper, ma'am. You're going to need to look at me, and show me your driver's license."

The woman with her head and arms on the steering wheel didn't move, in response to Daniel's request.

He couldn't see her face at all, couldn't tell how old or young she was, or what she looked like. Dark hair with gleaming golden lights fell around her head and onto the wheel, as effective as a deliberate disguise. He could see the frame of her dark glasses, but on a summer afternoon those were hardly a sinister attempt at concealing her identity.

She seemed a little on the thin side, the knobs of her backbone visible through a stretchy cream-colored top, as well as the faintest outline of a light blue bra. Below that, she wore a filmy patterned skirt.

She was in her twenties or thirties, he decided. The skin on her hands was smooth and soft. Her nails were neat and clean and bare of polish. The clothing looked clean and summery and of good quality, suited to the late-model car she was driving and the warm July afternoon. A chunky purse lay on the floor in front of the passenger seat, and a bottle of water had rolled against the seat back.

Nothing out of place, except for the fact that she didn't move.

He assessed the situation. She could be on the point of passing out from drink or drugs. She could be mentally ill. She could be working some kind of a scam, luring passing motorists to stop and offer help, at which point her accomplices would appear out of the undergrowth for a gunpoint robbery. Daniel had been a hospital security guard in New York City for three years, then a police officer in New York and a state trooper here in Vermont for a total of five. He'd seen all of these scenarios and worse.

"Are you ill, ma'am?" he asked, after weighing the wording of the question in his mind.

"Yes, a migraine. A bad one."

"I'd like to show you my ID."

"My vision is blurred, and I'm having a dizzy spell. I can't see."

"In that case, I'm going to have you feel the insignia on my shirtsleeve. It's a double chevron. I want you to know that I'm an officer of the law." Leaning down to the open car window, he kept his eyes on the screen of shrubby trees beyond the shoulder of the road, waited for the sound of slurring—either real or faked—in her voice.

She reached up, found his shirtsleeve and felt the raised weave of the insignia, rubbing neat fingers across the fabric, brushing his bare upper arm with the heel of her hand just below the hem of the short sleeve. The touch was accidental, yet oddly personal. "Okay. Thanks," she said. "I do believe you."

"Do you need medical attention, ma'am?"

"Yes." If she was faking, then she was good at it. If she was impaired by substance abuse, it didn't show.

"I'll call the ambulance," he said.

"No, that's…not necessary. Not an ambulance."

First indication of something not quite right. He went on high alert. If the "dizzy spell" was bad enough that she really couldn't move, then why didn't she want an ambulance?

But she was speaking again. "Call my brother."

"Your brother?"

"He's a doctor. Andy McKinley. He lives just a couple of miles from here. He'll come get me."

Daniel knew Andy quite well. Doctors and law enforcement officers tended to know each other in a rural community like Radford. There was a connection between hospital emergency rooms and crime, and he and Dr. McKinley had been involved in various incidents together. Andy was a good guy. Understood the police angle. Went the extra mile. Didn't let any ego get in his way. Daniel would almost call him a friend.

He didn't let on to this woman right away that the name was familiar, however. In his experience, personal information was best handled on a need-to-know basis, and he considered that most people needed to know very little about him.

Some people—work colleagues, and his sister, Paula, for example—said that this showed in the way he talked, and the way he often paused before he talked, but he didn't care and he wasn't prompted to change.

Andy's sister would learn of his connection with her brother soon enough. No sense wasting time or words over it now. "Andy McKinley," he echoed, giving nothing away. "Can you give me his number?"

Obediently Scarlett reeled off the digits of Andy's cell phone, then heard a moment later, "Andy? It's Daniel Porter, here."

What?

The name ambushed Scarlett from out of the past. She couldn't take it in, couldn't react. Daniel—that other Daniel—had grown up in Vermont, somewhere near here. Indirectly, two steps removed, that Daniel Porter was the reason she was here, now, although he wouldn't know it, and she hadn't thought of the Vermont connection herself in years. Hadn't thought about Daniel at all, except for the maddening fact that he wouldn't stay out of her dreams.

But now he was here.

Because it had to be the same man.

She couldn't know for sure, since the blurred vision meant she couldn't look at him and his voice wasn't enough to go on, but it had to be him. This man had said he was an officer of the law, she'd felt the insignia on his shirt and she knew that a law enforcement career had always been Daniel's goal.

It had to be him.

She waited for a whole slew of possible emotions to wash over her—anger, regret, embarrassment, self-doubt and loss—but none of them came. She was simply too shocked.

"I have your sister here," he said into the phone, "pulled over on Route 47, just coming in to town." He listened for a moment, then said carefully, "No, nothing like that. She's been taken ill, and she's hoping you'll be able to come get her." He listened again. "A dizzy spell, she says."

"Put him on," Scarlett managed, on a croak.

She felt the hard, cool shape of a cell phone pressed against her cheek, and the softer touch of a masculine hand. Daniel Porter's hand. She scrabbled for the phone, managed to take hold of it and the hand went away. She made another attempt to open her eyes but the bright light whirled in a sickening way and twelve steering wheels danced like dervishes right in front of her.

Don't try it, Scarlett, just breathe. "Andy?" she got out, after a moment.

"Scarlett, you sound terrible. What's the problem?"

"Migraine. Vision problems and dizziness. I had to pull over. I need you to come."

"I can't," Andy said blankly. "Not right now."

Before she could stop herself, she let out a stricken sound.

"I have a patient under local anesthesia, and four moles

to take off her back. I practically had the scalpel in my hand when you called. After that, okay? *Immediately* after."

This time, she couldn't keep back a moan. His voice had made her feel as if help was at hand, and now it had been snatched away.

"I'm sorry," her brother said. "I can't blow off a patient."

"I know." Scarlett wouldn't have done it, either. She rounded her lips and blew out a careful breath, gaining enough control to tell him, "You're right."

"Listen, Daniel is a good guy. Straight down the line. A state trooper."

"Yes, so he said." Andy hadn't met Daniel, six years ago, even though, indirectly, he'd moved to Vermont because of Daniel's influence. He had no idea that Daniel and Scarlett had briefly been involved. Almost no one knew that. Their whole relationship had vanished into the past without trace.

"He'll call an ambulance for you. He'll wait with you till it comes."

"I don't need an ambulance. It's just a migraine. I've had these spells before."

"Like you're having now?"

"Never this bad."

"So the hospital—"

"Don't make me go to the hospital." She was so overdosed on hospitals. She'd been working ninety hours a week in one for years. She was the smartest one in the family, Dad always said, but somehow that didn't seem like the best end of the deal when her skin always smelled like chemicals and she only ever saw the sky through tinted glass. "I just want to be lying flat in a dark room."

"Put Daniel back on and I'll ask him if he can drive you to my place."

"My car…"

"He'll drive your car off the road, park it somewhere safe. One of our office staff can drive it home for you later."

"Home to your place."

"Home to my place, it's no problem, it's not far. Put Daniel on."

Blindly she held out the phone, gripping the wheel with her free hand to minimize the movement. "My brother wants to talk."

A hand took the phone. "Sure," said the gravelly voice. Daniel had been twenty-four years old when she'd known him, to her twenty-six. He must be thirty, now. His voice had deepened, matured, but he was as measured and careful with his words as he'd always been.

"Yes, I can do that," he said to Andy after a moment. "Give me the address." He listened. "Yeah, no problem. I had court, this morning, in White River Junction. Was on my way back, done for the day. It's no trouble."

"Thank you," she said weakly, after she heard him put away the phone.

"No problem," he repeated. "We'll get you home, Charlotte."

Charlotte... Andy must have said her name, only Daniel had heard it wrong. He didn't know who she was. The thought came with a wash of relief. Maybe he wouldn't even remember.

No, he had to remember. He'd brought her up here, six years ago, had given her a passionate, romantic weekend in a gorgeous bed-and-breakfast, and then she'd dumped him two weeks later—or they'd dumped each other, she wasn't even sure—because...

Well, just because.

Too many reasons to count, and maybe she was ashamed of some of them, or maybe they weren't all her fault. They'd both had issues that ran deep. They'd both had reason to be angry...and full of regret. She hadn't been involved with another man since. She'd been burned, and it had been all too easy to retreat into her demanding work and conclude that the thing with Daniel—its intensity and its failure—was a warning sign.

He had to remember.

But right now, he wanted her to move, to climb out of the vehicle. He had one hand on her elbow and one on her shoulder, trying to ease her out from behind the wheel, trying to help her, but it was going to be impossible. She felt incapable of walking, and she couldn't have corrected him about her name even if she'd wanted to.

And she didn't want to, because...

Well, just because.

Because it was easier not to have him know who she was.

Not yet. Not until she'd reached a safer, better place than the verge of a county road.

Five and a half years ago, she'd sent Andy to the same bed-and-breakfast that Daniel had brought her to, at a time when Andy had been going off the rails due to stress and ambition. Her brother had found Vermont so good for his soul that he'd moved here, but that little leapfrogging connection wasn't relevant now.

She doubted that Daniel had looked at her face yet, and might not recognize her even if he did, she must look so wretched, white-skinned against the contrast of the dark frames of her sunglasses. Oh, and she'd been in her blonde phase six years ago, too, the style of it perky and tousled and a lot shorter than it was now.

"Can you help me to your car?" she asked him. "I'm so dizzy."

"Of course," was all he said.

She waited for him to hold her shoulders or reach for her hand, hating this feeling of disorientation. Where was he? Which part of her body would he touch first?

Okay, here was his arm coming around her shoulder…and his other arm sliding across the backs of her knees. He was planning to carry her. He lifted her into his arms before she could protest, settled her closer against his body, and then she had to concentrate so hard just on breathing that she couldn't say a word.

He didn't speak, either.

She was pretty light, but she was still a grown woman, and this had to be hard for him, but he gave no sign of it, just held her and paced toward his patrol car, his stride as smooth as he could make it. He was trying not to bounce her and she was grateful for that.

Grateful for his shoulder, too. She couldn't hold her head up without dizziness and wild color strobing behind her closed lids, and his shoulder was the only place to rest her cheek. There, she could smell the summer-heated cotton of his shirt and something nutty and fresh and masculine that was probably shampoo or aftershave.

It was good, the male fragrance. It was *familiar,* heaven help her. It brought a tangle of powerful, seductive memories, yet still somehow steadied her senses so she kept breathing it, drawing it in through her nostrils in slow pulls of air, while her hair fell across her face and tickled her mouth. She wanted to ask Daniel if he could brush the hair away, but still didn't trust herself to speak—let alone to make such an intimate request.

Touch my hair. Touch my face. You've done it before…
No.

Daniel Porter was carrying her in his arms like a knight rescuing a maiden and his strength and his movement felt so nourishing and good, yet he had no idea who she was.

By the time she was seated inside the patrol car, she felt weak with the aftermath of the short journey. She would have to see if Andy could find something stronger for the migraine pain. These over-the-counter pills were barely taking the edge off. She had to lean against the dash to anchor herself so that the whirling universe would slow down. Once more, her hair hung around her face, hiding skin that must be paper-white by this point. She couldn't even speak enough right now to say, "I'm sorry."

Daniel didn't seem to need the apology. "It's okay," he said, just as if she had managed the words. "It's fine. You're not heavy." The tone was friendly, professionally reassuring, with the same measured carefulness she still remembered so well.

As if words were too powerful, sometimes, and might detonate an emotional bomb blast if you spoke too many of them, or if you said the wrong ones.

"Just sit for a bit," he continued. "I'll open the windows so you have some air." She heard the humming sound of the glass lowering in its frame. "Your keys are still in the ignition, right? Just nod."

But with her throbbing head, speaking was easier than nodding. "Yes."

"I'll pull your car over, farther from the road." He made a momentary pause, then added, "That's why I thought I should stop and check on you, before, on my way through. Your car isn't pulled off to a safe distance."

"I couldn't."

"I understand that. It's okay. It's a quiet time of day."

Daniel Porter left her, and she sat with closed eyes and her forehead against the dash and listened to the sound of her car being moved. He was back in a couple of minutes, putting her purse carefully into her lap through the open passenger window, below the stiff forward angle of her upper body, and guiding her hand to close around the keys he gave her. "Got them?"

"Yes."

"Anything else you needed?" A pause. "I'm sorry, I should have asked before."

"My bags are in the trunk."

"Right, okay."

"But they can stay there until Andy organizes to get my car to his place. Did you lock it?"

"Yes, I did."

"Thank you."

Poor woman, Daniel thought, as he pulled onto the road. When he'd carried her, every step and every tiny movement he made had seemed to worsen her dizziness and pain, and she'd felt too light and limp in his arms, with her head pillowed on his shoulder like that.

He really would have preferred to take her direct to Mitchum Medical Center, but her brother was a doctor and hadn't insisted on the need for urgent medical attention, so he deferred to the expert opinion.

Dr. McKinley's house was only a mile or two from here, in the oldest part of the town, a street of grand old Victorians dating from when nearby marble quarries gave Radford a vibrant economy. The street had gone through a period of decline at one point, and Daniel vaguely remembered from early in his childhood that some of these places had been pretty run-down, divided into cheap apartments or lived in by families who couldn't afford to keep them maintained.

They weren't run-down anymore. He passed a bed-and-breakfast place, an architect's office, an upscale hair and beauty salon, each with a professionally painted sign swinging on pieces of chain hanging from a wooden stand planted in the lawn.

Dr. McKinley's wouldn't have a sign. Which of the elegant houses was it? He had the number, but glanced sideways to see if his passenger might point it out.

She wouldn't.

Couldn't.

She still had her head pressed onto the dash, with her forearms folded above. As he'd noted before, she looked too thin, as if she hadn't been eating properly or as if she burned all her calories in stress. Suddenly there seemed something familiar about her. He couldn't place it, but realized that he easily might have seen her up here before if coming to visit her brother was a regular thing.

No, he thought. It wasn't that kind of familiarity. It had been triggered by seeing her beside him in the car, as if he'd had her as a passenger in his vehicle before.

He couldn't think about it now...2564...2570... This was Dr. McKinley's house right here, nicely done up but not too feminine or fancy. Cream and dark green paint, newly stained timber on the front porch.

He turned into the first of two driveways. "Do you have a key to your brother's house?"

"No, but I know where he keeps one. Could you...get it for me?"

"If you tell me where it is."

She described the location, somewhat less obvious than under the doormat or sitting on top of the frame. Fourth planter pot to the left of the driveway, under the dark gray rock. She waited in the car while he unlocked the front door—the big Victorian was divided into two apartments, and he guessed that Andy's was 2572, not 2572A—then he had to come back to help her out. She clung to him and leaned on him as if he was the only fixed point in the whole universe, but at least she was walking on her own, this time.

Suddenly, holding her in his arms once again, recognition came. It elbowed its way past the changed hair color and style, the pale face beneath the large sunglasses, the weight loss, and came fully into focus.

It was Scarlett.

Scarlett Sharpe.

Shoot! Damn! It really was!

Scarlett Sharpe was Andy McKinley's *sister?*

Daniel didn't know if she had recognized him. He thought she was probably in such bad shape that she hadn't. He must have said his name to Andy, but had she been listening? Had she made the connection? Did she remember? What had he said? Too much?

He felt a wash of anger and embarrassment and regret and yearning and vivid memory, as well as a sense of unfinished business. He fought to keep any of it from showing then realized that she wasn't going to be picking up on those kinds of emotions, when she was struggling to take one step in front of another.

"I can't leave you alone here," he said, trying so hard to keep the reluctance from coloring his voice, so that it ended up sounding completely wooden instead.

"Andy won't be long."

"All the same."

"I'm okay. I just need to drink some water and lie down."

He was torn by a level of uncertainty and indecision that didn't happen nearly so often anymore, but which had once been very familiar. How much to give away? How much to trust? What to offer? What to say?

He'd been twenty-four years old when he and Scarlett had known each other before. Six years on, twenty-four seemed like it was just a couple of years beyond boyhood. In so many ways back then he'd been older than his years.

In other ways, far out of his depth, with his emotions so powerful and simple that they frightened him.

Lord, he didn't enjoy some of those memories…

Which was good, because memories weren't relevant right now.

"I'm going to wait with you until your brother arrives," he told her, making a decision he didn't intend to change.

Scarlett didn't reply.

They made it up the steps and through the door. "Where do you want to go?" he asked.

"Couch." Apparently because she didn't think she could make it any farther, even though he was carrying her again.

He helped her to lie down, finding a red silk pillow for her head. "Could you close the drapes?" she asked weakly. "The light is so bright."

It wasn't.

Not to his eyes, anyhow.

But he did as she'd asked, and it seemed to help her. She lay with her eyes closed, still wearing her sunglasses, and less tension stiffening her thin frame. She'd had more weight on her six years ago, for sure. He remembered how her body had felt in his arms, and it hadn't been scarecrow thin like this, it had been lush and soft, almost plump in places. Recognition might have come sooner if she hadn't changed so much.

"Can I fetch you the water you wanted?"

"Bottle or tap, I don't mind. A big glass. It'll help."

He went through the adjacent dining room and into the kitchen and ran the faucet into a glass he found upturned in the dish rack, not wanting to check in the refrigerator or open the kitchen cabinets in someone else's house. When he brought the filled glass back to her, she said in a thready voice, "Is it okay if I don't try to sit?"

"It's fine." He brought the glass awkwardly sideways to her mouth, and it was such a personal action it gave him the jitters. Would she want this from him?

She seemed to prefer the drops spilled down her cheek to the thought of movement. "Thanks. You can go now. Please. Don't feel you need to stay."

Did she know who he was?

There was no reason for it to matter, not when she could barely move, and he wasn't going to ask, or tell her. Not yet. Not unless it seemed truly necessary.

"I'm not leaving."

She stayed silent for a long moment, as if assessing his determination, and whether to protest. Finally she told him, "Thank you."

And then they just waited.

Chapter Two

This was Andy now, thank heaven. Scarlett heard his car, then the thump of hurried feet up the steps and onto the wide, wraparound apron of the porch. He barreled through the door and into the front room. "Daniel, thanks so much for staying. Scarlett, how're you doing?"

"A little better," she said, putting some chirp into her voice. "My vision is the main thing. Really can't see."

"Can I take a look?" She heard him sit on the coffee table in front of the couch. Daniel must be hovering in the background. She couldn't hear him. They'd been silent together for probably fifteen minutes or more before Andy had showed up. She hoped Daniel put it down to the fact that she was feeling so bad. Hoped he still didn't know who she was. But really she had no idea. She wasn't in a position to discern anything about what he was thinking or feeling. He'd never been a man of easy words.

Right now, she was just glad that Andy was here.

"Open your eyes," Andy ordered.

She did so, to be greeted by blurring and multiple images and blinding light.

"Your pupils aren't contracting," Andy said. "That's why it feels so bright. You're not focusing at all."

"Tell me about it!"

There was a pause. "Still biting your nails, Scarlett?"

"What's that got to do with anything?" But she hid her raw-tipped little fingers in the curl of her hand, self-conscious.

"Migraine can be stress related."

To head off a lecture, she just blurted it out. "I resigned, okay?"

"You *what?*"

"I resigned from the hospital." She had to talk carefully and quietly, or her head hurt too much. "Dad doesn't know. He thinks it's just a vacation break. I'll have a month here, as planned, but I'm not going back to City Children's."

"When will you tell him?" Andy knew as well as Scarlett did that Dad wouldn't approve the decision.

"When I've worked out what I'm going to do next."

"And you haven't, yet? You have no idea?"

"That's what the next month is about. I know he's going to kill me. Or not speak to me for five years."

"Wow."

"What?"

"I didn't think you'd actually do it. Thought you should. Didn't think you would."

"Neither did I." She was a little scared about it, too. Was she giving up medicine completely? Giving up pediatric oncology? She didn't know. All she knew was that being the smartest one in the family wasn't making her happy, the way Dad was so sure that it should.

"Is a month going to be long enough?"

"Don't know that, either." Who was she, if she wasn't a doctor? Who did she want to be?

He wasn't going to let the subject go. "Do you have any concrete plans for how you're going to spend your time up here?"

This one, she could answer with confidence. "Woodwork."

"Woodwork?"

"I want to learn to do something with my hands, something practical and creative." Something sensual, almost, but she didn't feel comfortable using this word out loud. Wood? Sensual? It sounded weird. She went on, "But I'm not—you know, much into fabric or yarn. I've been in contact with a man up here, Aaron Bailey, who makes fine furniture and he's happy to have me as an unpaid intern for as few or as many hours a week as I want."

"Scarlett, that's great!"

"I know." *No, don't nod. It's painful and dizzying.* "I'm looking forward to it. I'm giving myself a few days and starting with him on Monday. I've told him I'll start with sweeping shavings off the floor and just see how far I get. Maybe it will tell me something about my life."

"Seriously, Scarlett, I think that's a really great idea!"

"Thank you," she drawled at her brother. "I do have them occasionally."

She registered that Andy had said her name a couple of times now, and that this time Daniel Porter couldn't possibly have misheard, as he was standing in the room, probably looking right at her. Even though he hadn't said it, he must know who she was, despite the fact that she was thinner and had long ago abandoned her brief exploration of short and blonde.

Did he know that she knew him? Did he know that she knew that he knew that she knew?

It was more dizzying than the state of her brain.

It was weird.

"I'll get a stronger painkiller for your head," Andy said. "And what do you feel like eating? I can go to the store."

"You're driving down to the city this afternoon," she reminded him. "I'm supposed to be moving in next door, to your vacant rental, not collapsing on your couch and having you take care of me."

"I can postpone the trip till you're feeling better. I'll head down tomorrow or Saturday."

"I'm not letting you do that. Claudia is expecting you. She needs you. She *wants* you. Go today."

She knew how important the trip was to him. He'd worked the past two weekends in a row, covering for colleagues who would in turn cover for him, for the next six days while he went to New York to spend time with his girlfriend, Claudia.

Claudia was starting back part-time at work this coming Monday, three days a week, and despite this reduction from the full-time hours she'd once planned, she was very jittery about leaving her three-month-old baby in day care. Andy wanted to be there for her, there for baby Ben, and then they would both come up here again next Thursday before Claudia needed to head back to the city the following Sunday afternoon.

Yeah, it did sound overcomplicated.

Since Claudia was the best thing that had happened to Andy in a long time and he was quite adorably in love with her, if you could ever consider an older brother adorable in any context, Scarlett absolutely did not intend to ruin their plans.

She didn't think this dividing-their-time-between-New-York-and-Vermont thing was going to work for them for long. Not when there was a baby involved. And she couldn't bear the idea of being responsible for them having less time together, instead of more, until they worked out a more concrete future. They were exploring several options, she knew. The one thing they were both certain of was that they wanted to be together, and to make it work.

"So you'll manage on your own," Andy said, delivering the words with a heavy dose of sarcasm.

"I'll be fine in a few hours." But she knew this was too optimistic. Her last migraine, less severe than this, had required two days off work. She'd spent a further day gritting her teeth and pushing her way through the aftermath of a weak body and a woolly brain. Being here on her own, even with stronger painkillers, wouldn't be fun.

Silence from Andy.

She could feel his hesitation. He wanted so badly to be in New York, this minute or sooner. "I can't leave you on your own yet." The words dripped with reluctance. "I could see if Mom could drive up and—"

"Not Mom." Because then Dad would get involved, and Dad didn't believe in stress-related migraine, not in the McKinley family. And she absolutely didn't want to have him find out yet that she'd left City Children's Hospital, because she knew that even if he understood and forgave her at all—and she was sure he wouldn't—he would still push her to make decisions about the future right now, and she knew she wasn't ready.

McKinley medics were invincible, as far as he was concerned, and Scarlett didn't want to have to confront him on the subject until she was actually *feeling* invincible. With answers. And certainty.

Dad had reacted badly enough to the little she had said. He'd spent weeks trying to talk her out of this break. As the youngest daughter and only girl, she should have been the one he spoiled and doted on, and okay, she was, but

Dad's form of doting had always been a little different. IQ tests and puzzle books and mathematical challenges, prizes for perfect grades, summer science camps and father-daughter museum trips. She'd felt all the love and pride and pressure, and she felt it still.

"And anyhow, Mom couldn't get here before nightfall, so you'd still lose nearly a whole day," she told her brother, with difficulty.

Daniel Porter hadn't said a word, but now he cleared his throat. Scarlett heard a creak as he shifted his weight. "I can stay till she's feeling better, Andy."

"I can't— I don't—" Andy began.

"Listen, what are we talking about? The rest of today? Overnight at most? I don't have to be back in court till ten tomorrow morning. And I owe you over that arrest back in March."

"That was professional. This is personal."

"Might not get the opportunity to return a professional favor for a while."

Andy went silent again. So did Daniel.

Then Andy's phone rang.

Claudia. Even in her impaired state, Scarlett could hear the heat and softness in his voice. "No, there's been a delay," he said. "I'll be a little later than I wanted, I'm so sorry." He listened for a moment, then controlled a sigh. "Hopefully before dark."

He'd made the decision. It was settled. Daniel Porter was staying.

"Yeah, me, too, can't wait..." Andy said. He was grinning, she could tell. He ended the call and his tone changed. "Dan, thanks. I *really* appreciate it. Can I make a list of errands? I'll pick up the script for her medication and drop it back here, but if you could shop for something to eat?"

"Whatever you need," Daniel said. "Scarlett—" he cleared his throat again, and again she heard a floorboard creak as he made a shift in his weight "—help me make a list."

He most definitely knew who she was. It was clear, now.

He felt as awkward about it as she did, she could tell even with her eyes closed and her head throbbing, and the fact of her migraine was almost *convenient* in masking the odd, complicated feeling in the air, but it still wasn't enough. "Soup," she said. "And toast."

"Yeah, let's talk about what you'll need to do." Andy sounded so much more cheerful, in a hurry to get everything sorted and take to the road.

"For a start, her car," Daniel answered. "I can head back to the station and get someone to drive me down to Route 47. It's not far. Then the store. I'll run home and change, too, grab a couple of things."

"Okay, let's check what I have on hand." Both men began to move, heading toward the kitchen. It was a relief to Scarlett to be left on her own, with their voices in the background, working out the details.

"She can sleep here tonight," Andy said. "Doesn't make sense for her to move next door to the rental apartment, where the refrigerator and pantry are both empty." Scarlett heard the sound of his refrigerator door opening as he checked its contents. "We need milk and bread."

"I'll write it all down."

"This is great, Daniel. I really appreciate it," Andy repeated. "When you don't even know her…"

Oh, but he did.

He stayed silent about it, and so did she.

Andy left after about five minutes, apologizing to Scarlett and Daniel and thanking them all the way out the door, saying he'd drop the medication in before he left for the city, probably in an hour or so. They both listened—or at least Scarlett assumed Daniel was listening—to his car backing out of the driveway, and then another eerie and uncomfortable silence fell.

"Please turn on the TV," Scarlett eventually said.

"What would you like to watch?"

"Nothing. But you must be getting bored."

"I'm reading. Found some crime fiction."

"Right, okay, then, sorry." He must have given the book a flourish, because she could hear the riffle of the pages.

"You should try to rest, shouldn't you? Sleep?" She heard the creak of the adjacent armchair where he must have sat down.

Sleep was a thousand miles away. "I'll try," she lied. Time passed, stretched out and endless the way it had seemed in her car before Daniel had stopped. "Please can we have the TV?" she said at last. "I need the distraction."

She heard him stand. "Sorry," he said. "I didn't realize."

"It's okay."

He picked up the remote, swore under his breath a couple of times as he pressed the wrong buttons, but then the sound came on. She heard snatches of music, gunfire, voices shouting, canned laughter, a newsreader's measured words, and guessed he was surfing the channels. "What do you feel like?"

"Keep pressing. Stop for a little on each channel. I'll tell you."

He surfed some more. How many channels did Andy get? She heard weather and more news, a cooking show, an old Western, then Angela Lansbury.

"Stop there," she said.

"Murder, She Wrote?"

"I've probably seen it." Every episode, at least three

times, late at night while winding down from a heavy on-call or a heart-rending session with the parents of a gravely ill child. She'd watched most every detective series over and over. "I can fill in the visuals from the dialogue." She liked the old-fashioned, family-orientated crime shows, the less graphic and confronting ones, the ones with a nice twist and a lovable sleuth and a satisfying ending, nothing too confusing or clever or challenging. Comfort food on a screen.

"Okay. *Murder, She Wrote*, it is."

"Sorry, it's probably a lot less interesting than your book."

"I'm not really getting into the book. So it's fine."

"Thanks."

"No problem, Scarlett."

I know you know I know.

But still they didn't say it, and she felt horribly out of her depth about it, because of the fact that she couldn't see.

Daniel had caught the beginning of the episode. After a few minutes, she recognized which one it was. The one with—

"Well, what do you know?" he said. "That's George Clooney!"

Yes, she'd remembered it right. George wasn't the murderer, just the clean-cut love interest for one of the other characters, mugging in the background with a top-heavy mop of 1980s hair.

"Funny where people start, isn't it?" she said, before she thought. "And where they…end up?"

"Yeah, it is."

Like the two of them, right now, in Andy's house, with her unable to look at Daniel or move.

You know I know you know.

But we seem to be agreeing not to say it, now.

"Can I get you anything?" he asked. "Andy has fixings for a BLT, or grilled cheese sandwich."

"No, thanks. Just…more water?"

"Of course."

He went out to the kitchen and refreshed the glass. She opened her eyes and could just make out the dark, blurred bulk of his figure on its way through the door. She'd forgotten the size of him, and the big shoulders. She closed her eyes again, thinking that maybe, blessedly, the brightness had grown a little less extreme.

A minute later she heard him bend down to her, heard the sound of his clothing shift and slide against his body. His knuckles pressed lightly against her cheek while she took the same awkward sips as before, and something familiar came to her senses, a charge of awareness and need that she shouldn't be feeling when her vision still churned and her head still pounded like this.

What did he look like now, beyond the blurred, broadshouldered silhouette she'd been able to glimpse?

She had a sudden, powerful shaft of memory, from the first time they'd met, six years ago, and for a few blessed moments, the memory managed to override the migraine.

In her mind, she was back in the E.R., examining a child complaining of stomach pain, adding up the symptoms and thinking it didn't look good. Even though the pediatric E.R. beds were in a separate area from the general beds, she could still hear the commotion nearby. A detoxing addict had turned abusive and violent. This one was apparently stronger and more persistent than most.

She finished her exam, and promised the parents that the senior doctor would be there soon to order some tests, then she left to return to the pediatric medical floor on level six…

And there was Daniel, strong-shouldered and intentionally intimidating in his uniform, responding to a call for security. She passed him just as he reached the knot of people caught up in the addict's drama—passed him close enough to almost brush his arm, which was flexed big and hard beneath the dark gray shirt. Close enough to see the control and determination in his face.

Some security guards didn't look like that. They looked as if they enjoyed the prospect of wielding power and force a little too much. They practically grinned in anticipation as they approached a potentially violent scene. Daniel, in contrast, seemed calm, businesslike, implacable.

Incredibly good-looking, too, in a way she didn't usually notice, with his angular features and well-shaped head, close-cut dark hair and matching stubble, deep-set black eyes and powerful size. Until that point, she'd always gone for very smart, cerebral men, liking their intellect before she noticed their body.

Daniel was different, that first day and every day afterward.

Daniel was so, so utterly different from Kyle, the ex-husband whose last name she'd still been using back then. She was powerfully aware of it from the very first moment, when he glanced sideways at her and then ahead to the scene that awaited him.

She couldn't help the turn of her head in his direction, couldn't miss the moment when their eyes met, heard him say to the addict a moment later, "We're done here," and then that was it. She reached the swing door that led out of the E.R., pushed it open and left. The backward swing of the door blocked out sound and sight. She never learned the aftermath of the addict's behavior, and the child with stomach pain turned out to have leukemia, which eventually went into remission and then cure.

Her first sight of Daniel Porter was the thing that stayed

with her, and she must have given something away in her face or her body language… She must have been more naked than she knew. Because he began to smile at her when they passed each other in a corridor or met up at a desk. Soon, he was saying hi and pausing to talk.

The conversations grew longer, and he didn't seem in a hurry to bring them to an end, even though the subject matter was usually pretty trivial and sometimes he seemed to find talking a challenge or an effort, and then one day—

Yeah.

A drink. A meal. Bed.

She was so horribly on the rebound at that point, from the ugly unraveling of her marriage. Kyle had remarried so quickly, it had felt like a studied act of revenge. Maybe it was. Kyle was like that. She would never have taken him back, and she wondered about the new wife, but still her emotions from the breakup were raw.

Maybe the reason she'd responded to Daniel so strongly was purely that he seemed so polar opposite to her ex, in so many ways.

But you couldn't make a relationship work when it was based on choosing the opposite to what you'd had before. And with the painful timing, it could never have worked with Daniel, no matter what kind of a man he'd been. They'd both been crazy even to try.

Chapter Three

Was Scarlett asleep?

Daniel wasn't sure.

She hadn't moved or spoken for a while now, and her breathing was very even. It was almost three o'clock, and Andy should be back with the prescription pain medication any minute. The TV was spewing out another crime show rerun. He preferred hospital shows for when he needed to unwind in front of a screen.

There was a symmetry about it, he realized. Scarlett was a doctor and liked TV crime. He was a cop and liked TV medicine. Neither of them wanted to revisit their working environment in their time off.

Healthy.

Something in common, too, in an upside-down kind of way.

Only problem was that this particular TV crime show was killing him with its implausibility.

He tried to find in Scarlett's face and body the same woman he'd known six years ago, but couldn't, and maybe that was good. She'd been quite defiantly blonde back then. Now her hair color was a natural golden brunette, but that wasn't the biggest difference.

Where were the big, liquid, intelligent brandy-brown eyes and the sensitive, full-lipped mouth? The softness and curves? Lost in fatigue and stress and weight loss and pain. He'd eventually recognized her, but only just, and even now he couldn't put his finger on what had finally clicked. Not her voice.

Something harder to define.

Something—and this appalled him, when you got down to it—that had its source in his memories of her body when they'd made love. The way she'd closed her eyes and surrendered so totally to the moment. The way she'd moved. The way she'd been possessed by the strength of their physical connection to the same degree she was now possessed by the blurred vision and pain.

They'd only been involved for a few weeks, but he hadn't known sex like it before or since.

He hadn't known certainty like it before or since, either.

Hell, what kind of an admission was that? What did it say about his life? Was this why he hadn't said anything to her about their past acquaintance? Because he was afraid that his memories of their time in bed, and his memories of how she'd made him feel, would color his voice and she would hear it? Because if they talked about the past, then she might guess how much he'd never gotten her out from under his skin?

How could you say a calm, casual, "Remember me?" in a situation like this?

Better—*way* better—to let it go and say nothing.

For now, at least.

* * *

Scarlett began to feel human again when the stronger pain medication kicked in at around six o'clock. Andy had brought the pharmacy bag into the house, grabbed his overnight bag and left for the city almost at once. After she'd taken the medication, Daniel had left for the store, and now she could hear that he was back. He still had the key from under the flowerpot, and when he let himself back in the house, she heard the rustle of the shopping bags.

He closed the door behind her, put down the bags and came through into the living room, to Scarlett's couch. "What can I do for you next?" He sounded like a cop, again. Voice deep and clipped. No words wasted. No hesitation or doubt.

"Find another crime show before I murder one of those designers…"

He didn't laugh. Well, okay, she wasn't being that funny. Humor was all in the timing, and hers had disappeared along with her vision. She heard him pick up the remote and start channel surfing, stopping at the first show he came to. She listened to it for a moment, then they both spoke at the same time.

"Sorry, I can't handle—" from her.

From him, "Sorry, do you mind if we—?"

"Please," she agreed. "Switch."

"Sitcom?"

"One with an audience, not canned."

"Let's see what we have here… And then can I heat you some soup?"

"Please."

She managed to sit and sip soup from a mug, in between bites of toast that Daniel had rested on a paper napkin, and when she opened her eyes the multiple images had resolved down to two, the blurriness was lessened and the light didn't hurt anymore. She still couldn't see clearly, but the progress felt good.

Daniel came and took the empty mug from her hands without her having to ask.

"Thanks. I'm feeling a lot better, painwise, even if the vision still isn't that great."

"You're looking better. Way better color."

"The soup really helped."

"I can heat you some more."

"Actually, yes, another mug."

"More toast, too?"

"Please. It's really settling my stomach. How come you're so good at this?" she blurted out.

There came a long beat of silence, then, on a reluctant growl, "My mom was sick for a long time. From when I was a kid."

A shock ran through her. He'd never told her that, six years ago. Never once. Not hinted at it, or—

Nothing.

She'd worked out that he'd had a challenging history— well, he'd ended up rubbing her face in it, with deliberate anger—but she hadn't known about his mom. He'd never told her enough about anything, back then, and it shocked her that he hadn't breathed a word about something this huge.

"She died a few months ago," Daniel added, in answer to the question Scarlett hadn't found a way to ask. "It was a good thing, by that point. She was glad to go."

She apologized awkwardly, as if it was her fault that she hadn't known. Maybe it was. Maybe he would have told her about his mom's illness when they'd come up here, if—

Yeah. If a few things.

If she hadn't been so obviously on the rebound. If her ex hadn't left her with so much emotional baggage. If she hadn't been so scared of the strength of her physical response to Daniel, when her whole life her bright mind was the thing she'd been taught to rely on. If she'd had more trust—because she hadn't trusted even the good things about him, back then, let alone the obvious differences between them.

And if they hadn't spent so much of their short time together in bed.

"It's okay," he said, and the words covered all sorts of bases, and allowed them both to let the subject go.

Silence wasn't comfortable, though. She scrabbled around in her woolly mind for something to say, but Daniel managed it first. Very polite. "Your brother has done up the house great."

"It's gorgeous, isn't it? He didn't do all of it. The previous owner had made a good start. I've seen some photos from the 1970s when it was a dump. Badly subdivided, with cheap paneling everywhere, and dark brown paint with mustard-yellow appliances and flooring."

"I remember that kind of color scheme. Actually our refrigerator was avocado-green."

"You're not that old!"

He laughed. "Some people don't manage to buy a new appliance or repaint a room for quite a while after the fashions change."

"True." She held her breath. It was the kind of conversation topic that would have deteriorated into an argument six years ago, hinging on his underprivileged background—living with bad paint—and her well-paved path through life—regularly updated decor. She would have said too much, made it all too complicated, while he would have said barely anything at all, but with a sense that there was enormous emotion lying underneath.

Would he turn it into an argument now? Or one of the white-hot, simmering silences she'd hated?

After a moment, he laughed again. "Funny how you can turn memories around."

"Yeah?"

"I hated those paint colors when I was a kid. Now they're an anecdote. A war story."

"Kids today think they have it tough," she mimicked. "*We* had to live with avocado-colored refrigerators."

"What is it they say? What doesn't kill you makes you stronger."

"It surely does!"

They talked a little more, never openly confronting the fact that they knew each other, but letting it say itself in a reference here and there. Daniel held himself back, the way he always had. Scarlett gave a little more, and felt a zing of triumph every time she got something from him in return.

She thought that they couldn't have related to each other like this in any other situation. It was only happening because she couldn't see, because he'd had to help her, and because there had been that first ten or fifteen minutes when it wasn't clear whether they both realized that they'd met before.

After a while, the conversation petered out in a natural kind of way. They watched—or in her case listened to— TV in silence, while she measured the passage of time in sitcom units and listened to Daniel's occasional gruff gurgle of laughter.

She liked it when he laughed. It was a warm and very physical sound, reassuring and hopeful. Laughter created companionship every bit as much as conversation. Maybe more. She laughed along with him a couple of times, and his laugh touched her like a soft blanket or the palm of a comforting hand. She wished the sitcoms were funnier, so that the laugh would come more often.

Four and a half of them went by, which meant that it must be around nine. They'd spent most of an evening together and barely said a word, and yet she felt her emotions settling to a deeper place, a better place than she would have thought possible, with regard to this man.

For the past six years she'd felt a churn of uncomfortable memories and feelings any time she thought of him. She'd second-guessed everything she'd said and done, and everything he'd done, too. Maybe she hadn't needed to feel that way. Maybe none of it had been as bad as she'd thought, on either side.

Well, huh.

She let the thought sit, didn't know what she wanted to do about it.

Time for more medication, and the bed awaiting her upstairs. He brought the pills to her, with a glass of water, and she gulped them down. From experience, she knew that it didn't do to let the pain take hold again between doses. The medication was most effective if she stayed strictly to the four-hour interval.

"Thanks, Daniel."

"No problem. Going up now?"

"That's the plan." She stood.

And swayed.

Light-headed rather than actively dizzy, maybe because she'd been lying down for so long.

Daniel was there almost at once, grabbing her by the elbows and then, in case this wasn't enough, stepping right up to her so she could grasp two fistfuls of his shirt and lean her weight into his chest. When she took a staggering step sideways, he kept her on her feet, and then the light-headedness subsided and she felt almost normal, apart from her sight.

He put his arm around her waist and engulfed her hand in his and it felt good, even though she couldn't even see him, she had no idea what he really looked like now. Not in detail. If he had lines starting to form around his eyes and mouth, or if his hairline was receding, but he felt so good, and he smelled so good, too, like sandalwood and mint and clean laundry.

"I could make you a bed on the couch, if it's too hard for you to get upstairs," he said.

"I want a real bed. It's worth going up for."

"Yeah, a real bed is always good."

The words dropped into the air and seemed to hang there. She remembered the big, puffy four-poster at the bed-and-breakfast. She remembered the bunk bed in the doctors' on-call room at the hospital, when Daniel had wedged a chair under the handle of the door.

She remembered her own bed at home in her parents' Manhattan apartment. She'd gone back there to live after her separation from Kyle and had stayed on there through her demanding internship year, until she had more time to find the right place on her own.

Mom and Dad had been away for the weekend. Daniel had looked around at the high ceilings, the oil paintings on the walls, the windows with a distant view of Central Park, and couldn't hide that this level of privilege was new to him and troubled him. What did it say about their differences?

But in her bed together, that hadn't mattered.

In her bed, nothing had mattered except the way they moved together, the way they made each other feel, the sense of discovery and magic, the blissful contrast of his big, strong body and her softer, smaller one.

The only thing they'd ever really had during those short, intense weeks—sex, and bed, sleeping wrapped in each other's arms.

It had scared her with its overwhelming power.

"Are we doing okay to move?" he asked. "Steady?"

"Yes. Thanks."

But before they could start the walk toward the stairs, he added quietly, "We should say it, don't you think? We've both been holding off." He took a careful breath, and she could feel it through their contact. "You remember me."

"Of course I do." She opened her eyes, but they still wouldn't focus properly. He was just a darker blur in a fuzzy radiance. "Even though I can't see you."

Sight was overrated, her body said. Neither of them moved. Time slowed. The heat of his hands burned into her and she felt the air seem to thicken around them. She could have let him go and stepped away, but she didn't. Neither did he.

"You're not blonde anymore."

"That was my divorce hair." She could feel the way his chest expanded and contracted as he breathed, could feel the detail of ribs and abs and back muscles beneath the cool weave of a short-sleeved T-shirt.

"You never wanted to talk about your divorce." She knew the sleeves were short because the soft inner skin of his arm was in direct contact with her forearms as he closed his body more protectively around her. "I think you mentioned it twice."

"We weren't all that much about talking, you and me, were we? I still don't want to talk about it."

"It was that bad?"

"No, it was more… The marriage was that bad."

"That's not why we fell at the first hurdle, the two of us—because you'd had a bad marriage."

"No. One of the reasons."

"The other reasons… I never really understood what they were," he said slowly. He loosened his hold a little, creating a slow friction where their bodies touched.

"You were angry…" she reminded him.

"So were you. And you pulled right back. I could feel you pulling back, and so I pushed harder and it all got worse until you just cut off."

"The timing was wrong. Everything was wrong."

"Without giving me a chance to bridge the gap. The last thing we ever did was go to bed."

"Are you still angry?"

"Are you?" he countered quickly.

She bit back a retort that this was what he'd done before, he'd always turned things onto her, made her talk first and talk longest, so that she was the one who had to put herself out there, put her needs and feelings on the line, at a time when she was still such a mess from her marriage.

It was true. He had done that.

But there were so many mistakes and faults on both sides, she couldn't untangle the rights and wrongs of it. It had been a mess. If she forgave herself, then she had to forgive him.

She said some of this, haltingly, and *felt*—because she couldn't see—the way he listened. Cautiously. Willing to hear. Resistant about some of it. Tightening his hands at one point, and then softening them against her back. "I agree it was both of us," he said. "I agree that we can't just…be angry. Anger is such a prison. It holds you back. Even when you can see it, you can't help it sometimes. But let's not."

He spoke as if he knew from bitter experience, driving home to her once again how little they'd really known about each other. She didn't know what had happened in his past to make him believe anger was like that, did things like that.

"Is anger what you've felt, if you've thought about me, over the past six years?" She tried to open her eyes again, saw a shimmery blur. He was too close. She couldn't bring him fully into focus and it threatened to make her queasy. Best not to look.

"No, mostly not," he said. "You?"

"No. More like a sense of inevitability. I've thought about it. I could never find a way for it to have been different. We just weren't in the right place, either of us. Me more than you, maybe?"

"Don't know about that. But yeah, neither of us in the right place. Lot of regret. Not much clarity."

"Pretty much."

He shifted his weight again, and she felt the pressure of his chest against hers. They didn't speak. She remembered what she'd decided after Daniel—that she really wasn't cut out for the whole *love* thing. It was too daunting. Too huge. Too much of a contradiction to everything she'd been taught about her own strengths.

She'd had one failed marriage, and one failed fling where even the great sex couldn't hold them together for more than a few weeks. The great sex seemed like the problem more than the solution. It was deceptive. It got in the way.

Immersed in her work, she might have tried love again if it had come her way. She'd planned to be very careful about it, to take it slow, to keep sex safely out of it for as long as she could. But she'd never had to follow through on those plans because no man had seriously tried for more than a date or two. How likely was it, really, when she kept to such a tight, demanding routine?

Daniel was the first to speak again. "What about the reasons why it was good between us, Scarlett?" His voice dropped low and slow. "What do you think, now, about those?"

The air went still and heavy around them, while the past crowded in and their bodies remembered. She wanted to tilt her head and see if her cheek would find his shoulder. Or lean in and lift her chin. Her mouth would be sure to find something, if she did that. Something delicious and wonderful. She knew it, because he was so close. She would find the hard, satiny heat of his neck. Or the fragrant tickle of his hair. Or the tease of his gorgeous mouth.

A man's mouth didn't change in six years.

Her own body began to soften and swell and melt. Her skin was so sensitive, she was acutely aware of every inch of Daniel's touch, every ounce of pressure, every tiny sound he made, the strength that seemed to come off him in waves, like radiant heat.

"The reasons why it was good..." she said.

Incredibly, with her vision still below par, her capacity for arousal seemed to be working just fine. She shifted her weight, the way he had done a minute ago, and the movement brought their thighs together. He stood at a slight angle, so that one knee pressed between her legs, dragging her skirt into a deep fold.

"Yes. You know what I'm talking about. Have they changed?" The whole world narrowed to just this—her and Daniel, holding each other, remembering with their bodies what they were skirting around so cautiously with their words. "Has *it* changed? That one amazing reason?"

"How can I know?"

"You have an inkling." His hand slipped a little, closing

over her hip. She could feel the warmth, and didn't want it to go away.

"Okay, but that's a toe in the water."

"Is it? You can tell a lot from a toe. If the water's warm or cold. If it's clean against your skin." They both stood very still, and Scarlett barely managed to breathe. "You want to find out if this feels the same all the way?" His hand slid across and down and traced the curve from the small of her back, across her butt, to the top of her thigh. "More than a toe in the water?"

She answered him only with a ragged breath.

"This was always so good, Scarlett, *so* good. This was how it started. We got to this pretty soon. This was the center of it, the meaning of it. This was where it was always the best."

"Yes…"

"Yes!"

"But we stuffed it up."

"We stuffed everything else up," he corrected her. "We never stuffed this. Never once. We slept together on our first date and we never, ever got it wrong."

Chapter Four

Daniel heard himself sweet-talking—practically begging—Scarlett into bed and wondered what the hell he was thinking.

Start into this again? Risk losing himself this way? He didn't know if he should wish he'd never stopped beside her skewed car on the verge of the road this afternoon, or if he might count it as the luckiest action of the year.

His body had a pretty powerful opinion on the subject, but should he listen to it? His body told him he could have Scarlett in the palm of his hand with the right touch behind her ear, the right peachy softening of his mouth over hers, exactly the way he'd had her before, but how crazy would that be?

He couldn't believe how much he wanted her, even with all the baggage they had, all the memories of how it hadn't worked before. His body said none of that mattered. The past was gone. *Now* was what counted. But he knew that *now* didn't last, while its legacy often did.

It was like in a cartoon, with a tiny angel version of himself sitting on one shoulder and a tiny devil on the other. Talking him up. Talking him down.

"You can regret it in the morning, big fella," the tiny cartoon devil urged. "Now is now."

"She's worth more than a one-night stand," the cartoon angel insisted.

"Doesn't have to be one night. The regret might be weeks away. The regret might never happen."

While the cartoon symbols of his conscience bickered away, Scarlett made the decision for them. He could feel her body shaking beneath his touch, the power of her response that much stronger because she otherwise seemed so thin and frail with the pain and dizziness that were only just losing their hold. "Upstairs," she said. "In a bed." She took his hands and made them move down her body, the message that she wanted his touch so naked and clear. "Because I don't have a strong enough head for anything creative tonight."

"You mean—?" he began, slow about it in spite of her bluntness and her signals, not able to believe that she would make it this easy, even though she'd always made it easy six years ago.

She'd never used sex as a bargaining chip or a power play or a strategy. Not even right at the end. As he'd reminded her just now, the very last thing they did before she told him it was over was to make love with dizzying, almost desperate satisfaction, as if there'd been no problems between them at all.

"You're right," she said simply, with her palm cupped softly against his jaw and her whispered words just a fraction of an inch from his mouth. "We never once got this wrong."

He carried her.

Not because she needed it, the way she had on the verge of the road, but because the sheer, crazy charge of hearing her say that she wanted him had no place else to go. He just scooped her up and settled her against his chest and went for the stairs, while she tightened her arms around his neck and tried to control her breathing. "Oh, Lord, Daniel, how do you make me want this so much?" He felt so strong and full of triumph about what was happening that he practically laughed out loud.

It was so sudden.

So very much wanted.

Both of them.

Total equality about it.

He'd had to fight all evening not to keep looking at her and mostly it was a fight he'd lost. He'd watched her color slowly come back and her movements become stronger and less dominated by pain. He'd watched her sipping the soup and chewing neatly on the toast with her eyes closed. She'd kept her hands wrapped tight around the mug and he could see in her face that it made her feel better, even before she'd said so.

He'd watched her occasional attempts to open her eyes, the dark lashes lifting to show darker pupils before she'd made a frustrated sound and closed them again. He'd watched the careful way she talked. Their past relationship was written so clearly on her face, in good ways and bad, if only she knew.

He wasn't done with this, and she wasn't, either.

It was unfinished, six years ago.

Or it was finished wrong, which came to the same thing.

"I'm scared," she said.

"I won't drop you." Her butt was safe against his stomach, while her thighs and spine pressed on his arms, with such warm, satisfying weight.

"I'm scared of pretty much everything *except* you dropping me."

"You changing your mind?" They'd reached the top of the stairs. He lowered her down, the initial charge of his energy spent. They held each other almost desperately, as if their contact wouldn't be able to reconnect if it broke.

"No! But scared is part of it." She stroked his arm, sliding her hand beneath the sleeve of his T-shirt and then bringing it right down to his wrist. Her touch triggered a million nerve endings into a response. "Honesty matters in bed." She spoke as if she knew from experience. Different experience. Bad experience. Not what they'd had together. Her marriage, he guessed.

"It does," he agreed. He stepped closer, even though that was barely possible. "Honestly, then? I'm scared, too."

"Yeah?"

"Same reasons, maybe. That it won't be as good."

She laughed, hunched her shoulders and gave a shiver. "I'm scared of the opposite." She held on to the belt loops at his waistband as if she needed the support, and pressed her forehead into his shoulder. His jaw settled against her hair as if it lived there.

"What's the opposite?" He couldn't think straight. Her hand had come whispering across the front of his jeans. He wasn't sure if she even knew she was doing it. Her eyes were closed, the way they had been all day. She was so naked in what she gave away, when she couldn't see.

"That it'll be too good," she promised. "Mind-blowingly, terrifyingly good. And you'll reach into my guts and squeeze and I won't know where to go next."

"Did that happen before?"

"Yes. It did. And I don't know how much of that was because of…well, my marriage."

"Not a factor this time around."

"No."

"You squeezed my guts pretty hard, too," he admitted on a growl. "You nearly broke them. And you're squeezing 'em right now."

"Am I?"

"Yes. Hard. It almost hurts. It aches."

"Good," she said, almost fiercely. "Because I'm aching just as much."

He kissed her because he couldn't help it. Because her mouth was right there, so soft, with a tiny patch of dryness on her lower lip that he wanted to moisten with his tongue. She responded in an instant and they deepened the kiss with mutual need, couldn't get enough of each other.

He took her lower lip lightly between his teeth, softened it, stroked it, covered her whole mouth with his and felt the deliberate caress she gave back to him, and the little nips and tastes. Her mouth moved with velvety softness and he chased every movement, wanted it deeper and deeper and seriously couldn't, couldn't, *couldn't* get enough.

Sometimes a kiss was just a kiss.

Sometimes it wasn't.

This was one of those times.

This kiss *mattered* down to their bones.

And it was just the start.

The long, unhurried, magical start.

He was hard as a rock and straining against his jeans by the time she sighed and sagged against him and said on a thready breath, "You are amazing when you kiss."

"You, too."

She pulled on his hand, stepping backward along the

corridor, and he was once again afraid for her dodgy balance and turned her around so that she could lean on him if she needed to. Suddenly he thought about the need for protection, and put the problem into words on an awkward mutter. Shoot, how could you ever be fluent about something like that?

It didn't seem to bother her that he'd sounded clumsy. "Bathroom cabinet, I'm sure," she said. She pushed him in that direction, almost as clumsy as he was, and went ahead to the bedroom. He watched to check that she was steady on her feet through the open door, and the round side-to-side of her bottom with each step was such a distraction that he almost forgot why they'd parted company.

Oh, right. Bathroom cabinet.

He found the slew of packets he was hunting for and arrived back in the dark bedroom in time to see her in her pale blue bra, shedding her skirt to show matching underwear.

And he remembered.

She didn't wear bikini briefs or a thong or anything like that. She wore those soft, silky, satiny things that had a name he couldn't remember—the ones that were cut high and loose around the top of her thighs, making it so easy to slide his hands up inside and cup her sweet, firm butt.

He must have done that a hundred times, six years ago, even in just the few short weeks they'd had.

He wanted to do it again.

She had her hands at the elastic waist and he reached her just in time to whisper, "Not yet," as he stroked downward across the silk that curved over those so-female cheeks, and then upward between fabric and skin. Oh, man...

She squished against him, all soft and pressing and delicious, her breasts neat and round, with nipples tightened hard enough to graze his chest even through her bra and his T-shirt. He felt the impatient rocking of her hips and knew that she wanted this as powerfully and physically as he did.

It did something to him, sensing the way his body kindled her female fire. *Yeah, I can do this to you? Me? So much? Oh, that's good, because you do it to me.* He pushed himself against her, finding the swell of her mound through those slippery panties. Oh, they fit together so well.

He reached around and unsnapped the bra and she shimmied the straps off her shoulders and tossed the bra aside. She couldn't see where it landed, and he didn't care. Now for that satin-covered elastic at her waist. He pushed at it and it slid down and he let his hand brush deliberately across her soft curls as he went lower. She stepped out of the tiny pool of satin and he ran his hands all the way up her body in celebration of her nakedness.

Beautiful.

Belonging to him.

She'd always belonged so totally to him when they made love. Or they'd belonged to each other. It didn't make sense, it was just there, a deep, hidden secret like a vein of gold in plain rock. He'd believed in it totally in the moment. After they'd split, he'd forgotten. Or he'd distrusted his own memories.

Surely it *couldn't* have been that strong?

But his memories hadn't lied, and six years had changed nothing.

He pulled off his own clothing with clumsy impatience, after tossing a couple of those packets from the bathroom onto the end table beside the bed. T-shirt and jeans and boxers he just threw on the floor. Then they came together again. She'd been waiting for it, standing there, letting those eyes drift open—seeing his naked skin only as a pale blur, he could tell—and then shut once more.

"I didn't turn on the light," she said, brushing her mouth against his.

"That's okay. I'm guessing it still hurts your eyes a little." Downstairs, they'd sat almost in the dark, with just the light spilling in from the antique chandelier in the front hall.

"Much better than it was," she said. "If you want the light on…" She released her hold and slid onto the bed, on top of the covers, and lay on her back. Waiting. Smiling. Eager but half-blind. Lost and waiting to be found. By him. No one else.

"I like making love in the dark."

"You do?" She smiled wider.

"It's softer. There's always enough light to see what counts." He could see it all right now. She shifted her position a little, rolling half onto her side so that one breast fell against the other, creating a shadowy cleft. She darted her tongue over her lower lip and the bluish light coming from a lamp in the street outside showed the moisture.

"What counts? Tell me what counts, Daniel."

"Are you teasing me?"

"Yep."

"Are you really making me say it?"

"If you can stand it."

He could stand it. Just. "What counts?" He slid onto the bed beside her and took inventory, fighting for the best words. For the words that wouldn't ruin this. "Your body. Your skin. Your mouth on me. I like to see all of that. With shadows, and little gleams. Wetness on your lips." It had dried now. He wished she'd do that little kittenish lapping motion again. "What do you like to see?"

"The light and dark. Your eyes are so black. The contrast of your hair and your skin." She was still smiling. With her eyes closed, she looked as if she was dreaming in her sleep. "Your mouth is such a beautiful shape. Your mouth couldn't possibly belong to the wrong man. That doesn't make sense."

"Doesn't. And you can't see any of that, tonight, anyhow."

"I can feel. And remember."

But Daniel wasn't about memories at this moment, he was about now. Only now. He rolled against her, done with games and teasing and talk. He just wanted her mouth and her hands. He wanted the rediscovery. He wanted to know if the magic would be just the same.

It was.

It was better.

She came alive beneath his hands, her breathing ragged as he touched her breasts and laved them with his mouth. He couldn't get enough of her—the sounds she made, the electric, writhing response of her body. When she began to climax against his hand, she begged him to fill her, and when he did, pushing with a slick, almighty plunge, she met his thrusts with the pulse of her orgasm, sending him over the top with more speed and power than he'd remembered could exist.

They came to earth in a dark, steamy haze and just held each other.

In the moment.

Nothing but this.

Daniel was too scared to talk. They'd said the wrong things to each other too many times, six years ago. Sometimes he'd thought she did it on purpose, because she was scared and needed distance, and he'd never managed to keep his mouth from saying the wrong things back. Never in lengthy speeches. He just wasn't like that. But bad, pithy phrases that fell out of his mouth before he could hold them back.

He didn't want to start on any of that. He didn't want anything except this moment, feeling her in his arms, listening to her breathe, feeling the rightness of her and not asking questions about any of the things that could tear them apart.

Chapter Five

Scarlett slept until morning almost without stirring, and felt it was the most blissful, nourishing sleep she'd had in months. Maybe even years. The sun was bright in the room when she surfaced and she opened her eyes before she remembered yesterday's crippling headache, its causes and its effects.

But the light didn't hurt.

And she could see, with no double vision or blur.

Apart from a slightly washed-out feeling, she felt close to normal, and when she stretched in the bed with catlike thoroughness her body felt replete and good.

So good.

Except that Daniel wasn't lying beside her, the way he had been all night, his warmth or a whispered word lulling her back into sleep any time she began to waken.

She looked at the numbers on the clock radio. It was after nine-thirty. She must have slept for more than eleven hours. Daniel had a court appearance at ten this morning, she remembered. He would already be on the road to White River Junction. She saw a piece of folded paper propped against the side of the clock radio.

Didn't want to wake you. Hope you're feeling better. Court, did you remember? I should be back by five, to see how you're doing. D. Lower down the paper, he'd added, *You look so beautiful when you're asleep. I can't believe what you do to me.*

She felt beautiful, after last night. Beautiful and female and right with herself. It was a rusty kind of feeling. How long since anyone had made her feel beautiful, in or out of bed? How long since she'd felt *right?* How long since she'd cared?

It felt fabulous, and it felt scary. Which of those feelings did she need to listen to?

She climbed cautiously out of bed. A shaft of morning sun fell across the rumpled sheets, and she could hear birdsong, and a breeze ruffling the leaves of the huge old trees in Andy's backyard. The whole world seemed washed clean, and freshly bright to her vision. It was so good to have sight, and balance, and no pounding in her head.

She showered and found fresh summer clothes in her suitcase, smoothed out and hung up a couple of outfits in the closet on satiny padded hangers, went downstairs and poured some brightly orange juice into a faceted glass that glinted in the morning sun. Such simple, everyday actions but they seemed so precious this morning, washed new and clean and shiningly clear.

She didn't want to think about why—about how much of it was her body's thankfulness at being well, how much was Daniel and how much was being here in Vermont without the lung-crushing pressure of her work.

She just wanted to be in the moment, enjoy this loose, stretchy feeling in her body, let the blissful memories from last night wash over her. Oh, who was she kidding? So much of it was Daniel.

And it all worked fine, through a lazy day of sunning herself on the grass and rocking in the porch swing, reading a book. She needed more days like this. She needed to feel like someone other than a doctor, with all the pressure and responsibility and heartache that this entailed. She needed to feel like something other than the person Dad valued so much—the daughter with the highest IQ in the family.

It worked fine until four o'clock in the afternoon, when she sat down at Andy's computer with a steaming mug of coffee and two chocolate chip cookies and went online, with the thought that she'd catch up a little, check some Vermont sites and start thinking about how she was going to spend her time here when she wasn't at Aaron Bailey's studio. Maybe she and Daniel could eat out somewhere tonight. Maybe he could take her somewhere on the weekend. A picnic beside a mountain stream. A swim in a lake.

Better run through ten days' worth of email, first, and send a quick update to a couple of friends, because she'd been letting communication slide…

The email from her friend and fellow doctor, Kristin, jumped out at her from about a hundred others, most of which she could delete unread.

Kyle and Julie have split up, did you hear? Kristin wrote, while a gulp of coffee burned in the back of Scarlett's throat. She put the mug down. No idea what happened, she read on. Heard it third-hand via Steph Goldrick. Julie's gone back to North Carolina. He's apparently a little too well-adjusted about it to be real. As usual.

Thought I should tell you before you heard it elsewhere. You know, just in case. Xxx, Kris.

Just in case what?

What did Kristin think was going to happen? She couldn't possibly think—*nobody* could possibly think—that Scarlett would ever want Kyle back, or that she'd be pleased to hear that his second marriage had apparently failed. Even Dad, who'd thoroughly approved of Kyle for a long time, wouldn't have wanted that.

All the same, the news made her uneasy, especially the "just in case" part, and the "too well-adjusted to be real," and her sense of lightness and ease seemed shadowed now. Kyle always projected the *well-adjusted* thing. It was important to him. He fought so hard to be able to like what he saw in the mirror every day, but Scarlett had paid the price for that and she guessed that Julie had, too.

She shut off the computer, way more disturbed than she wanted to be, then heard the sound of a car in the driveway, and looked out a front window to find that it was Daniel, back a little earlier than he'd said.

The rush of pleasure hit uncomfortably against the darker mood left by Kristin's news about Kyle, and she remembered how it had been this way six years ago, too. The marriage was over, the divorce was final, Daniel was knocking her socks off in bed and out of it, yet Kyle was still a presence.

She'd heard about his engagement to Julie just a week into her relationship with Daniel. A month after that, hard on the heels of the disastrous weekend here in Vermont, she'd seen a photo from their wedding pinned up on a notice board in the doctors' break room at the hospital, and she'd known that Kyle himself must have put it there, or had a friend do it for him, as neither he nor Julie, also a doctor, worked at the same hospital as Scarlett.

How could he have gotten married again that fast? Didn't he need time, the way she did—the way the disaster with Daniel had *proved* she did—in order to change and grow and avoid a worse mistake the second time around?

Now that hasty marriage, too, was apparently over. She wasn't surprised. Kyle was a hard man to stay married to. There was *no reason* for her to feel uneasy about the timing, but she felt uneasy anyhow.

From the upstairs window, she saw Daniel cross the front garden in a few quick strides, to reach the steps up to the porch. He must have gone home to shower and change, because he was wearing jeans and a plain shirt, not the state trooper uniform she'd felt more than seen, yesterday. His energy jolted her out of the negative mood and she went down to him, heart lifting and spirits impatient.

He grinned when he saw the way she flung open the front door, that mouth showing his pleasure with its wide spread, and his dark eyes glinting with heat and satisfaction. "Better today?"

"So much better! I can't tell you."

"I don't have your cell number, or I would have called during our lunch break, to see how you were." His gaze roved over her, taking in that she looked better. He was clearly happy about it. The mood shone in him, created its own magnetic field that didn't translate to the words he used, which came out simple and plain, the way they mostly did. "We finished early."

"Do you have to go again?"

"Not for this case. This guy had guilt coming out of his ears, and today's witness nailed it. There's another one coming up next week. Traffic violation, serial offender. It'll go pretty quick, too."

"It's not like New York, I'll bet."

"Hey, just because we have mountains and trees,

doesn't mean we can't manage some serious crime once in a while!"

"You like serious crime?"

"I like getting it off the streets." He grinned again.

She grinned back and leaned against the door frame, suddenly weak at the knees—yes, it really happened—hit by a wave of...she never knew what to call it, with Daniel. It was giddy delight. It was like being drunk on air. It was fluttery and billowing and wonderful and important, a secret treasure that nobody else could touch or see. It put her in touch with a side to herself that she almost couldn't believe was really there.

It had scared her six years ago, and now she discovered that it scared her still, just as much. It was too powerful, without a direction or a name. She *needed* a name, if she was going to keep seeing him, if she was going to feel any sense of understanding or control. She'd been taught to value the precision of names. But there didn't seem to be one.

"I thought we could do dinner, if you're feeling up to it," he said.

"I had the same idea."

"Fancy or—?"

"Not fancy," she added in a very different tone. "And not yet..."

Had she really said that? Had she really said it with such unmistakable, seductive, suggestive meaning?

Daniel had *noooo* trouble understanding what she meant. His eyes lit up. He was grinning *again,* and they couldn't look at anything else, just each other. Her insides did that lurching thing. It was like the weak knees, it shouldn't be real, but it was. She wanted him so much it messed her up all the way through. Her whole body seemed to be made for him, like a lock and a key, and it was fabulous and she was so, so scared of it.

Because it didn't fit.

It didn't fit with anything she'd been taught about the way life should work. If something didn't make sense on paper, how could it make sense anywhere else? If you couldn't explain it, how could it be real? Dad had always pushed her on things like that, from when she was probably four years old. "Explain it to me, Scarlett," he'd say. Or, "Find the logic." And usually she *could* find it, and *could* explain, and she would know she'd made Dad happy.

There was no logic today.

And yet the wanting won out so easily over the fear, when Daniel looked at her like this.

He backed her across the porch with an arm thrown around her waist, stopping twice to kiss her, and bury his face in her neck. He smelled fresh and clean, the way a man smells when he's showered especially with a woman in mind. He hid nothing—not the light in his eyes or the impatience or the greed for her or the bulge at the front of his jeans.

Inside the house, he touched her body as if he'd owned it for years, and the confidence of his hands and mouth did something to her. Did even *more* to her. How could he touch her like that? How could he know just where it would feel good? How could he be so honest about it, no games, just wanting her and feeling great about it and letting it show?

"You going to move in next door sometime soon?" he muttered, the words smushing against her mouth.

"Tomorrow, I thought. Why?"

"Because when your brother gets back this kind of thing won't work. This is his place. I'm not standing naked in his kitchen."

You're planning to stand naked in my kitchen? Oh, I want that...!

"Definitely tomorrow," she vowed.

"I'll help shift your stuff across. I know it's not far, a couple of doors and half a porch, but don't try to do it all yourself. You looked so wrung-out yesterday. Your brother is worried about you."

"He worries too much."

"Still... We can shop some more, too, anything else you need me to do."

"Are you staying tonight?"

"Unless you're kicking me out."

"You know I'm not doing that."

He laughed.

And then he put some serious time into kissing her, and she almost forgot how to speak or breathe.

You could learn so much about a man from the way he made love. You could *relearn.* Daniel was exuberant and tender and generous and adventurous. He told her on a hot breath, "Like that," and listened when she said it back to him. *Yes, like this. Yes.* He told her what he loved about her body. The neatness of her breasts, the color of her nipples, the wispy hair at the back of her neck, the way she smelled, all over. He whispered in her ear, tender and dirty at the same time, and she loved the gravelly note of need and naked emotion in his voice.

When he made love to her, she loved everything about him.

They surfaced at seven, sated and breathless and hungry. She was so glad he'd already promised to stay here tonight, because now the possibility didn't need to be skirted around, with both of them afraid to make assumptions.

She lay on the bed watching him get dressed, and loved that, too. Loved the way he tried to get into his jeans too fast like a kid impatient to play, and had to hop on one leg, yelping and laughing at himself when he almost fell. Loved the way he grabbed his discarded shirt and pulled it over his head without undoing the buttons.

He noticed. "You're watching." He stood there and folded his arms across his chest, so that the honed muscles went hard.

"You're putting on a show."

"Funny kind of show," he said, bending to scoop up his socks as if they were tennis balls.

"Yep. It is. It's cute. Do the hopping again."

"You can't create a move like that, it just happens. Are you putting on a show for me?"

"Do you want one?"

"Surprise me. For later. Later is when I want the show."

"We're talking underwear, right?"

"We are. And anything else that you think of."

"Yeah?"

"Movements to match the underwear."

"Fling a wisp of lace across your bare chest?"

"You could do a lot worse…"

The sun was still bright and it was going to be a beautiful summer evening. They went to a family-run steak house a couple of streets away, with a small European-style beer garden out the back. She'd eaten there twice with Andy and her parents, but Daniel was greeted like a regular and when he asked for a table in the shadiest corner, they were led out to it right away, and promised microbrewery beers coming right up.

"Do you want beer food, to go with these?" Daniel asked her, when they arrived.

"You mean wedges and wings?"

"They do some pretty good nachos here, too. Spicy."

"Nachos and wings? Spicy is good."

"Spicy was very good, just now. I need to tell you again how much I like your underwear. It is so accessible."

"Accessible?"

"Did you not notice me accessing a few things with an impressive amount of smooth?" His voice was a slow tease.

"I thought that was just you, not the underwear."

"Okay, then we were a great team, you, me and the underwear. I look forward to our next opportunity for refining our procedures."

Their server approached for their order, in time to hear a line that could have suggested a serious business meeting. Scarlett told Daniel very soberly, as if they were both wearing corporate suits, "My team and I look forward to it, too."

"Which team? The pale blue one? Or the coffee?"

"Our top team, Team Black, whom you haven't even met yet. I think we could create an impressive track record, there."

"I'll look forward to that, definitely. Is there a Team Scarlet?"

"There is…"

"That could actually be our top team, I'm thinking."

"I'm sorry, I can come back in a few minutes," the server offered.

"No, we're ready," Daniel assured him, and reeled off their casual selections.

They'd worn out the conversation, with that last bit about the teams of underwear. Some beer slipped down, bubbly and light. Scarlett liked the way Daniel drank, gulping a mouthful, sighing his satisfaction, putting the glass down. He made it last, and didn't hurry to order a second.

"Do we need to decide on a name for this? A definition?" he asked quietly, out of the summery silence, when the beer was almost gone. He reached across the table and took her hand.

"For tonight?" She knew he didn't mean just tonight.

"For…" He hesitated. The words weren't there. Or if they were, he didn't want to say them.

She spared him the difficulty. "I'm sorry. I know what you mean. I don't know why I'm trying to make you say it. Because I can't, either." It was just what she'd thought earlier, too, when he'd first arrived after his day in court, that they needed a name. Something to call this. A summer romance. Casual dating. "I'm only—"

"Fobbing me off."

"No. Shoot!" She thought for a moment. "Fobbing myself off, maybe."

"Yeah?"

She took a breath, knowing it was time to bite the bullet. They couldn't just go on riffing about underwear teams and pretending they knew what was happening, and what was possible.

Say it, Scarlett. "We messed it up, before. And it wasn't fun. The contrast between the—between what we had in bed, and the rest…"

He answered slowly, "We were different people, then. In a different situation."

"Were we?" She honestly didn't know. What would Dad think about that? "Different enough, to the people we are now? Different in the right ways, our situation? Does it count?"

"That weekend…" He leaned closer, looked down at their joined hands, rubbed the pad of his thumb over her knuckles in slow strokes. She squeezed, as if to say, *Yes, do that, it's good, it's a connection, let's keep the connection.*

"Yes, can we talk about that weekend?" she said. "We need to."

How? She sensed it wasn't going to be easy. The noise level in the beer garden was rising. It wasn't a big place. Hard to tell if the other conversations going on would be a protection or would force them to talk uncomfortably loud.

She stretched forward, almost knocking down her beer, so that their heads were close. Listening distance. Debating distance. Kissing distance, almost.

Almost, but not quite. She could watch his mouth but she couldn't reach it. It was set in a serious line, his top lip seemed a little fuller than the lower one. Then he frowned and tucked his lips in at one corner and she wanted to reach out and smooth the little fold of tension away.

"Do you know," he said, after a searching moment, "that furniture maker you're going to be interning with, Aaron Bailey, he lives a mile up the road from my place? You'll go past, to get there from your brother's house." He sounded reluctant about it.

"I don't even know your place. And I haven't been to Aaron's yet, we've only talked via email and phone."

"My mom's place, really. Her family place. The place I grew up, my whole life. Except those five years I was in New York. I'm living there until we can sell it. My sister, Paula, is coming soon, to help sort things out."

"You never said anything about your mom," she reminded him carefully. "I never knew till you mentioned it yesterday that she was ill, while you were growing up. I'm sorry that she died before I could meet her."

"I had a whole plan, that weekend, to take you to meet

her. She was all prepared for it. She was waiting." He shook his head. "And then I had to tell her it wasn't happening, because you wanted to head back to the city."

"You never said," she repeated. "How could I know? I couldn't read your mind. I think we're pretty good at reading each other, sometimes, but there are limits. There were definitely limits."

"I know I never said."

"You seem to be blaming me for your mom's disappointment."

He let out a slow, tightly controlled sigh. "I'm sorry if it's coming across that way. It's not what I mean."

"So why didn't you tell me?"

"I was building up to it. Seeing if I could trust you. Easing you in slowly."

Those weren't good words. They didn't sound brave or trusting. They sounded manipulative and negative, a judgment on her. She couldn't control her reaction. "Easing me into what? To the fact that you didn't have a privileged childhood? To the fact that your mom was sick? You thought I was the kind of person who needed to be *eased into* that, sneakily, just because I was raised in a better situation?"

"Yes," he said. He'd narrowed his eyes and stuck out his strong jaw, and looked stubborn and angry, the way she remembered him looking six years ago. "Not sneakily. Not that. I don't like that word. Just slowly. I thought you'd have problems with where I'd come from. And my obligations. Which weren't going away. Which got worse, after Mom got sicker and Paula and Jordan couldn't be around to help."

"Daniel, I don't think I gave you reasons to think that way." It hurt. It shocked her, even now. It felt like a slap in the face, a kind of reverse snobbery, a proof that he hadn't had—or still didn't have—any idea who she really was.

Even when he seemed to know exactly who she was in bed.

How was that possible?

"You forced me to react badly," she reminded him. "You threw it at me. You made it happen. You did that horrible tour."

"Tour?"

"Yes. You have to remember."

"It wasn't a tour."

"It felt like one. First stop, this is where I used to collect bottles and cans for the deposit money, when I was seven. Second stop, this is where I got beat up and had the money stolen when I was nine. Third stop, this is where I found my dad unconscious in the gutter, when I was twelve, after he lost his latest deadbeat job and got drunk and passed out and fell down."

"It all happened, Scarlett." Their hands were still locked together. "It wasn't a *tour*." He looked up at her, his eyes narrowed and searching and furious, seeming to speculate and turn in to study his own responses at the same time. "That wasn't its purpose, for heck's sake!"

"It was. Felt as if it was. You told me about it in the bluntest, harshest, most confronting way you could."

"I'm not that great with words, sometimes."

"Deliberately, that time. You're good with words, when you want to be."

"Plain."

"There's nothing wrong with plain. That time, you used it. To hurt."

"To hurt myself."

"Maybe. In part. You weren't sharing your childhood with me, you were throwing it at me. Like mud. And then you dared me to look down at you for it, or run a mile, or brush off my clothing as if you were dirty. I seriously felt like I hadn't given you any reason to believe I would react that way." She felt shaky about the confrontation and the memories, and queasy at the disconnect between everything they had in bed and everything they didn't seem to have when they talked about some of this stuff.

"But you did react that way," he said.

"I reacted badly. Yes. I did. I couldn't take it, I knew the timing was wrong. In me. And for you. And I ditched the whole thing and told you to take me home. I reacted to your anger, to your trying to prove a point with a kind of violence."

"Violence… Sheesh!"

"Aggression. Emotional aggression. Kyle was like that." She thought for a moment. "Okay, no, different. Emotionally dishonest. Just lacking. But it came to the same thing. Or it was what I feared. Talking that went nowhere or went wrong. Emotions I couldn't get a grip on."

"I'm never going to be emotionally dishonest." The words came on a growl. "That's a promise. Don't think I know how. Emotionally clumsy maybe. Clumsy in how I say it."

"Is that what was happening?"

"Part of it. Those words aren't easy. Plain doesn't mean easy. My dad drank. We had no money. Those words are *hard.*"

"I didn't react to the fact that you had a dad who drank and struggled to stay in work. I didn't *know* you had a mom who was ill, because you didn't tell me. I reacted to the aggression."

"You made love to me after that, back in the city. We were practically clawing the walls."

Oh, she hadn't forgotten!

His apartment. The first time he'd brought her there. She'd barely seen it, couldn't remember a thing about it, could only remember the feeling of their lovemaking being a last-ditch stand. Ferocious and doomed. "I don't know what that was about. Both of us in denial? Both of us trying to fix things with sex?"

"Fix things with sex," he said.

She remembered vividly how hard she'd tried, how they'd kissed forever, touched each other everywhere, eaten each other up. "And then I realized that wasn't enough. That it was dangerous to depend on that. Too scary and wrong."

"It was the best night of my life, Scarlett."

Oh, it was. She still remembered. It still shook her. "All the more reason."

Their food arrived and they pulled their joined hands apart. Once again, the server had heard the tail end of the conversation, only this time it sounded nothing like a business meeting. Scarlett scooped some wings onto her plate and prodded one mechanically into the dish of sour-cream dip.

Daniel watched her. "So maybe we don't need a name for this, after all," he said. "Maybe it's a moot point."

"Because we've argued already?" She didn't know, herself, if they'd reached break point once again—shoot, so fast! "It's ending?" Her throat had grown a hard lump.

"Well, I don't want it to end," he growled. "That's the last thing I want."

"No." A hard, thick, scratchy lump. "Same here."

"Okay, that's something."

"I hope."

"But look at us. We're both angry. We're both harking back to all the exact same things that gave us all the trouble before. That we couldn't get past."

"And you think we can't get past them now?"

"Don't you?"

"No, because I feel safe," she realized suddenly, out loud. She put down her wing, uneaten. "I feel… I'm angry, but we're talking, we're saying it, and I feel safe about it. I'm not scared of you, or your anger, or mine. I want it said and honest, and then I want to get past it. I just feel safe."

"I don't get that." He reached across and grabbed her hand again, engulfing it between both of his, quite roughly, as if too much gentleness now would be dishonest. "Safe. Not scared. How are you not scared? Not scared to talk? Why does that matter?"

"Safe arguing with you. Safe laying it on the line. That's—" she shook her head "—strange. Good. It has to be good."

"It is. You're right." He let her go just as suddenly as he'd touched her and took a pull on his beer, and then they looked at each other helplessly.

Where were they now? Where did they go?

"Let's get this straight and on the table. Do you want to drop this?" he asked bluntly. "Do you want me to take you home and just say goodbye? Do you want to end it here and now?"

"No."

"Good. Neither do I."

So help her, she felt a rush of relief so powerful it almost brought tears. "Oh, shoot, Daniel," she whispered. She felt as if she was being knocked to the ground. Or lifted up to a cloud. How could you not know which?

"So I'm staying the night," he said.

"Yes."

"And we're going to make love till morning and not be in any kind of a hurry to nail a label to this, or solve all the problems, or say every word of hope or regret or anger or anything."

"I especially like the part about making love till morning," she put in, almost timidly. Was that bad of her? To feel that way? To ignore the fact that they'd moments ago been so much at odds, and focus on the shallowness of sex instead?

Was sex shallow in a situation like this?

"Yeah?" His voice was smoky, charged.

"Uh, yeah. Don't look at me like that or we won't even make it through the meal."

Chapter Six

He stayed the whole weekend, making the move with her into Andy's vacant rental apartment in the other half of the old Victorian, and there was an unspoken agreement between them that they wouldn't go near the serious stuff. Not yet.

They would rock the bed, but not the boat.

Oh, it was bad!

Was it? Wrong? Just stupid?

A part of her was so sure she'd live to regret it, because sex this powerful had to be dangerous.

The rest of her didn't care.

Team Black and Team Coffee showed tremendous potential for long-term employment. Daniel's performance indicators rose higher and higher. Scarlett's skill at handling manpower issues impressed everyone involved. They laughed and ate and lazed and slept, watched movies, drank wine, barely bothered to get dressed.

And the lingering fuzziness from Thursday's doozy of a migraine was chased away like a wolf into the woods. It wouldn't dare to come back for a while. When they weren't making love they were so lazy it felt like floating on a cotton cloud. She slept deeply in his arms, not just at night but during the warm afternoons, too, and felt so perfectly happy and cherished and safe.

On Monday morning, Daniel reluctantly tore himself away before seven-thirty, to return home for a shower, a clean uniform and a serious attempt at getting his brain back into focus. They'd admitted to each other that they were both going to have trouble with that.

Total, sated relaxation was a two-edged sword.

Scarlett waved him goodbye with a mug of coffee in her hand as he reversed down the driveway, watched him until his car disappeared down the street, and hated the thought that she wouldn't see him until tomorrow afternoon. He had an extended shift today, and she knew that Aaron Bailey was expecting her this morning at nine.

Having spoken to both him and his wife on the phone, she knew that the craftsman was an older man, somewhere in his mid-fifties, who'd dropped out of a corporate accounting career twenty years ago to focus on his love of working with wood.

She'd connected with him through her sister-in-law, Alicia, who had commissioned him to create a gorgeous maple wood dining table and chairs for the six-room Park Avenue apartment she and MJ owned in New York, thanks not only to his earnings as an orthopedic surgeon but his investments as well.

Actually Alicia's involvement seemed a little out of character, when she thought about it. MJ's wife was normally so cool and self-contained and private. This time, she'd been genuinely enthusiastic. "I love our table setting so much. To create a beautiful backdrop to good food is such a satisfying thing. Please do get in touch with him, Scarlett."

She was nervous as she followed the directions Aaron had given her, rocked by her all-consuming connection with Daniel and struggling to fit herself back into day-to-day existence. There was something else, too. What was it?

Make a right onto Whetstone Road, the final instruction read, *and the track into our place is near the top of the hill, on the left, about three miles along.*

Which meant that about two miles along, she would pass Daniel's place, according to what Daniel himself had said.

Was *this* the reason for the nerves?

Lord, yes! A big part of it, anyhow. She realized it as the very thought created a thump in her gut. Daniel hadn't been very precise, hadn't said which side of the road he was on. Aaron hadn't been all that precise, either. How far was "about"?

She was distracted, all the way along Whetstone Road, looking down to check the odometer as soon as she'd made the turn, looking down again at intervals to see how far she'd come. A mile. Now, nearly two.

The landscape was semirural, with houses and cabins and farms dotted in amongst open fields and bands of trees, and the suggestion of wilder mountainous country not far beyond. Some of the places she passed were neatly kept and prosperous-looking, with sheds or a barn, a handful of grazing horses. Others were run-down.

The odometer said she'd come just over two miles since the turnoff. Had she passed Daniel's place by now? On the right there was a neat little house painted a lurid aqua-green, surrounded by a stretch of manicured lawn too thickly covered in groupings of plastic flowers and painted concrete animals.

On the left, a ranch-style dwelling, with freshly stained timber walls and a new-looking deck wrapped almost the whole way around it, sat amongst a huge, sprawling junk-yard of old cars that appeared to have been there for years. There must have been a hundred of them, in rows and heaps or crowded beneath the roof of a few dilapidated sheds.

Neither place looked remotely like what she'd pictured as Daniel's childhood home. What would he or his ill mother be doing with all those cars? Would he really fuss with those brightly colored animals and flowers? Some of the plastic and concrete groupings looked very new.

So in that case, had she missed his place farther back?

"This is not why I'm coming up this road," she said out loud to the car radio, through a tight jaw.

She was angry with herself about her mental focus. She'd been going back and forth about the idea of taking some time off for months, and it had only been Alicia's rather left-field suggestion of working with Aaron that had pushed her to take concrete action, tell Andy that she wanted to use his vacant rental, put in her resignation at the hospital, make a solid commitment to her own well-being.

That migraine had scared her, four days ago.

She needed this break before she made any decisions about her future, and before she confronted Dad. She needed this exploration of a creative and practical side to herself that she'd never taken the time for in the past—that she'd never been taught to value.

Andy was right that she hid inside her work, and that she didn't need to have it consume her whole life the way it did. She couldn't afford to have it consume her, if it was going to destroy her health.

She wanted to change, and to find a better balance. She couldn't blow Aaron Bailey off, or throw Alicia's helpful and out-of-character negotiations with the wood craftsman back in her face, just because her much-needed break was turning into an interlude of wild times in bed.

"Near the top of the hill, on the left," she murmured, as a glance at the odometer told her she'd come almost three miles.

It was much easier to pick the Bailey place than it had been to identify Daniel's, back down the road. The graveled track that peeled off to the left was marked with a grouping of tall, carved tree trunks like totem poles. Below them was a carved and painted sign, reading Bailey Custom Furniture.

She made the turn, wound her way along a pretty, tree-lined driveway until she reached a clearing where a log home nestled in a green garden. To the left she saw Aaron's studio, a long, low, shedlike building with a gravel path leading around to a door at the side.

There was a woman in the garden. She straightened from her weeding when she saw Scarlett pull up near the studio, brushed her hands on her dirt-stained pants and walked across, her wiry mop of gray hair bouncing in its ponytail. "You must be Scarlett."

"Yes, that's right."

"I'm Judy, Aaron's wife," she said in a relaxed and friendly way. "He's in the studio. I'll take you right in, shall I? Then we'll have coffee."

"It sounds great."

The whole day was great, beginning with the richly brewed espresso, accompanied by Judy's homemade carrot-and-raisin muffins, and continuing through Scarlett's first tentative foray into working with wood. The studio had that wonderful aromatic smell of fresh-cut timber, and Aaron took her presence as naturally as if she'd been a delivery of ash or oak.

By three, she'd run out of steam and he told her, "Go home. You've done enough for your first day."

She'd swept shavings, tidied tools, cleaned equipment and been given her first project to try—a simple pine pencil box that Aaron promised her she'd have finished by Friday. She'd loved the rhythms of sawing and planing and sanding, loved that every action she did served to refresh the smell of the new wood.

"That is, if you're coming back," Aaron added.

"Oh, I'm coming back!"

Driving down the hill away from the Baileys' place, Scarlett looked again at the ranch house with the vast litter of junked cars, and the little aqua cottage with the riot of artificial animals and flowers.

There was something strangely alluring about the cars. Okay, so they were ugly and endless and they dominated the house's setting far too much, but they held the promise of undiscovered treasure. There were some that looked quite old, from the 1950s or even earlier, and she thought they would be a classic car buff's dream, the way a garage sale could be an antiques collector's dream. She began to hope, although she didn't fully know why, that this was Daniel's place, but there were no definitive clues.

What were the other choices? Farther on, there was a place with a sign advertising Sue's Scissortrix—Cut, Style and Color in my Home Salon, which didn't seem right. On the opposite side of the road, another house looked too new and bare. How accurate was Daniel's "about a mile"?

She was still thinking about it when she put her key in

the front door of the rental side of Andy's house and let herself inside. In her purse, before she'd taken three steps into the front room, her cell phone began to tinkle out its ring tone and she scrambled to find it in the mess before the message bank kicked in.

When she heard the familiar voice in her ear, she wished she hadn't tried so hard.

"Scarlett!" It was Kyle, she recognized his voice instantly.

"Kyle. Wow. I—"

"Been a while, I know."

"Yes, it has."

What else did you say? How else did you react except blankly, like that? The inkling of warning from Kristin's email three days ago hadn't done a thing to prepare her for this.

"I thought it was time we caught up a little," he said cheerfully. "How're you doing? Where are you, right now?"

"Oh, in Vermont, at my brother's," she replied vaguely. "I'm taking a break." She dropped her purse on the couch and paced through into the kitchen, while he asked more questions. How long was the break? Was she still at City Children's?

She gave answers that she regretted as soon as the words were spoken, even though there were no major revelations, nothing too personal. It was the kind of conversation she could have had with any colleague or casual acquaintance, and yet she didn't trust it.

"How about you, Kyle?"

She waited for him to tell her about his separation, but he didn't. He talked instead about his golf handicap and his recent professional successes. He'd gone into Radiology as a specialty, and was part of a thriving and extensive practice in lower Manhattan. He told her what he'd earned in the past year. "Not that the money is important, as such, but it's a statement, you know? It says something about the success of the practice."

"It does, yes," she agreed.

They chatted on. He'd been on a cruise recently. "The food was disappointing. It was billed as five-star, but not by my definition of the term." He'd read an interesting article about current thinking on treatment for Burkett's lymphoma in children. "What's your view, there, Scarlett?" He listened to her response, putting in a thoughtful, "Uh-huh," every now and then, so she'd know she had his full attention.

Eventually he said, "It's been great catching up," and she agreed and they ended the call, and it was perfectly pleasant and on the surface there was no reason for it to leave her with such a bad taste in her mouth and such an uneasy feeling.

Yet she had both, in large doses, and they dragged her back into a place she didn't like, and she couldn't shake it off.

"Daniel, it's me."

"Scarlett?" His whole body went on high alert, just hearing her voice. He was ready for her in an instant, like a medieval knight bound in honor to do her bidding.

"Yes." She sounded tense and abrupt and nervous. "I'm sorry to call you at work. We said we wouldn't see each other today, but…please come over tonight, if you can."

"I don't finish until ten." It was only four o'clock, now.

"I don't care. Just come. If you want, if it's, um, convenient," she added quickly and awkwardly, as if suddenly doubting her own intensity.

He couldn't have that. He didn't want her doubting anything.

"Oh, I want," he said.

"So—so come."

"I thought you might be out cold, by then."

"I won't be. I'm going to take it easy for the rest of the afternoon. I'd just…really like you to come over. Need you, if you want the truth."

"Need me?"

"Want you. In my bed."

She sounded upset. Or scared and jumpy. He couldn't quite pick it. Yet the emotion blasted down the phone line and he felt it in his own body almost as if whatever had happened to her today was now happening to him. If he'd been able to quit his shift early, he would have, but he was in charge of the station tonight and they'd had a couple of arrests.

Ten o'clock took too long to arrive. He handed over to another trooper who would work the night shift, changed out of his uniform and into jeans and a plain T-shirt at the station, then jumped into his car to head directly to Scarlett's.

She was waiting for him, hitting him right in the open doorway with that same blast of feeling. She stepped straight into his arms and hid her face in the curve of his neck, and he had to ask, "Don't you want to talk?" He tightened his arms around her and felt her warm body press hard against his. He felt a sense of belonging that shook him to the core.

"That's the last thing I want." She'd already turned her face up so she could kiss him, splaying her hand across his back, and he could feel the coiled tension in every gesture and movement.

"Seriously, what's happened?" It was hard to talk, with

her lips trying so hard to find his. She was doing it on purpose, keeping him quiet with her mouth. Normally he was happy about that. Words were so easy to get wrong. But tonight…

"Shouldn't we deal with it first?" he tried again.

She wasn't listening, just kissing. Her mouth drowned his words in honey and cream, and, so help him, how could he resist when he'd been thinking of this all day and half the night? Pictures and memories, the smell and taste of her, the sounds she made, the way she teased so saucily but never for too long, all of it coming back to him all day in bursts and flashes that he had to fight to forget.

She was so sweet and eager and hungry and fast. She pushed the door shut, pulled him in to the couch. The drapes were closed and the lighting was low. Her chocolate-brown lace bra pushed her neat, gorgeous breasts up and out, and when he peeled her top up from her waist and over her head, he could see the half circles of the tender, slightly darker skin around her nipples spilling over the edge of the lace.

He didn't know if *all* her underwear was this saucy but hoped to find out, piece by piece. She seemed to be enjoying the possibility just as much.

They were naked—or almost—within minutes, and he forgot everything. Even forgot that this had started because she'd called him sounding edgy and upset. The whole world narrowed to the feel of her against him and enclosing him, the rhythm they made, the way it built until it could build no more, and then just shattered and glowed like fireworks in a night sky.

They lay together on the couch afterward with their weight and warmth all pressed together and their breathing beginning to slow, and that was when he remembered. "What happened, Scarlett? This was escape sex." She pulled in a hissing breath and he knew the words had hit home. "And I need to know what you were escaping from."

She tried to laugh it off. "Escape sex was pretty good, I thought."

"Escape sex was amazing, but you need to tell me. It can't be so much of an escape that you never get around to talking about it at all."

"You're a fine one to say that, Mr. Motor Mouth."

"Okay, I know, I don't talk enough and you're right that it's important. So I'm turning that around on you. Otherwise it's not fair on either of us. Sex needs to be about us, not something else that I don't even know about."

She was silent, except for a sigh. She slid against him, nestling herself closer, like a puppy trying to find the most comfortable place amongst the litter. "Okay. You're right." She lay for another few seconds, building herself up to the thing she didn't want to say. "Okay. It's simple. My ex-husband called. He wanted to 'catch up.' It spooked me more than it should."

Daniel whistled. "Catch up? You've been divorced for six years."

"He's just separated from his second wife. I'd…heard that. A friend emailed, a few days ago. Kyle himself didn't even mention it."

"Yeah, that's a little strange. And you didn't tell me about the email."

"I didn't want to spoil the mood."

"There has been quite a lot of mood…" he agreed on a lazy drawl, and tightened his hold.

"I guess, when I think about it, I wasn't surprised to hear his voice."

"No?"

"It's the kind of thing he'd do. Regroup and see if there

was another angle he could play, as if relationships are a game of chess, with set rules and one goal."

Daniel's scalp tightened, and he said the words she was skirting around. "He wants you back."

"He never said that."

"Why else would he call?"

"I know. He never said it, but I think you're right, he was testing the waters."

"You didn't tell him to get lost?"

"When the whole conversation was so bland and polite? When he didn't even hint about anything like that?" She shivered in Daniel's arms, and he understood why she was spooked. She was waiting for the other shoe to drop.

"So what did you do?"

"Just talked, until he ended it. Then I called you."

"If I was trying to get you back, you'd know it. If I was telling your ex to go jump, *he* would know it." Daniel had visions of punching the man in the jaw, if they ever met. He had no plans to act on the visions, but they were pretty satisfying.

"I never had that honesty and simplicity, with Kyle. I never had that kind of rawness." She shivered again, and he felt the ripple of the movement as if the shiver was happening to him. "That was so much of the problem. He insisted on everything being so rational and controlled and verbal. We argued everything like a college debating society. Emotions never played a part. Those were way too messy and illogical for him. Our relationship was set up that way. The pattern was pretty strong. For a while I thought it worked. Dad always taught me to be proud of my mind. But I know now so well that it doesn't work. It's not enough, and it's wrong. And so I rebel."

"This was your rebellion," Daniel guessed. He cupped her hip, traced the curving shape of it, his hand moving forward and down to the crease that arrowed toward the satisfied moistness of her sex. The action was a kind of shorthand for everything that "this" could mean, and had meant already.

"Rebellion sex, then, not escape sex. Is—is that okay?"

"The sex was very okay. Unbelievably okay." He added slowly, "I don't want to think it's always going to happen for only those reasons. Rebellion and escape."

"Is that really how my body felt to you?" She traced little circles and patterns on his chest with the tip of a finger, like mystic writing. He felt his groin stir once more. "Only about those reasons?"

"No. Not at all."

"Good. I wish we were animals, sometimes. Somebody said it once. Or something similar. That words are given to us to conceal our thoughts. With Kyle that's not quite it, but…"

"What, then?"

"He uses them to paper over our feelings." She wriggled closer against him, still stroking his chest lightly as if she was only half thinking about it. Daniel lay almost forgetting to breathe, his whole being locked on to what she was saying, and what she was doing with her hands. "Or to pretend that we don't have feelings," she went on. "Or to make up for not having feelings. I used to buy into it, during our marriage. I kind of liked that he knew I was clever, you know?"

"It's pretty obvious you're clever. Trust me, I have to work to keep up."

"You don't! Well, it never feels that way."

"You should take your intelligence for granted, not feel needy about it."

"It was what he rewarded me for. Pretty much the only thing. The way Dad always did, too. The way Dad still does. And then it just got so bad. There was never anything else, never any gut response. I wanted to yell and scream and sob and laugh and risk and hate. I wasn't allowed to. Never ever allowed to. Those things were never given any—" She stopped, stuck for the right word.

"Validity," he suggested.

"Yes, that's it. That's the word. They didn't count at all," she agreed. "They were *dirty,* somehow. But I want them to count. I want my animal body and all its reactions to *count* for something, you know?" She tensed in his arms, as if she'd scared herself by saying it.

"They count for me," he answered softly, because it was true. Her physical reactions gave him the key to knowing her, he felt.

He loved the way her body reacted like a tuning fork, vibrating when touched the right way, singing for him. She seemed lost inside herself, sometimes. Back when they'd known each other before, too. As if there was a whole lot of stuff she was still sorting through, in order to work out who she was.

He thought it was pretty simple. She was smart and funny and beautiful and a good, decent, creative, perceptive person. She was female. She was strong. She connected with people.

Okay, so that list was getting pretty long, but there was nothing elaborate about it, nothing twisted or contradictory or out of place.

"Touch me again," she said.

"Yeah?"

"Please."

It was late, by this time. After midnight, probably. The house had cooled down from the summer afternoon heat. Bed would be way more sensible, but apparently she didn't want sensible tonight. She slid a little higher up his torso, deliberately rubbing her breasts over his chest, pushing those tight, cheeky nipples against his skin. She was still wearing the bra, which was a situation that had to be rectified, even though the bra wasn't accomplishing much.

Well, not as a garment, anyhow.

As a turn-on, it more than did its job.

Daniel thought they should probably cover a little more of the territory of Kyle, his phone call and whether the phone call was all the man had planned, but it seemed too hard and too wrong right now. "You want to stay right here?" he suggested, hearing the hoarse need in his own voice.

"I'm very comfortable. And impatient."

"Me, too." Without him planning it, his fingers came up to tease those nipples. The right one had spilled a little further out of the bra. Her left breast was just the tiniest bit smaller than her right. His hands had noticed each time they made love, lifting the subtly heavier weight of one against the other. He liked it. He kept having to check to see if his hands were right about the difference, from all sorts of angles. He thought she liked it, too.

Look how she responded when he brushed each nipple with the ball of his thumb. Look how she responded even more when he cupped her breasts and lifted them and used his mouth, teasing those pink buds with his tongue, making them harder.

Her eyes closed in bliss. "Oh, please... Oh, yes..." Her breathing went quicker. She arched herself against his cupping, caressing hands and wanted more.

"This?" he said, his voice going out of control, scratchy with need as he rounded his lips over those peaks and sucked for all he was worth.

"Yes." He moved higher to her mouth and kissed her, and she made the kiss harder and deeper, slower and wetter. And endless. Wonderful. Real. More real than anything they could say to each other right now.

Then she grabbed his hand and slid it down between her thighs before grasping him and teasing him into near-oblivion. She pulled him back from the brink just in time and he rolled onto her and drove into her, thrusting into the warm center of her until she threw her head back and moaned and called his name.

Oh, babe, that's right, that's what I want, to hear you say it as if it's magic.

He lost himself, tumbled over the edge and sank into her arms, and they both slept. He had his head on her breasts and awoke to find her stroking his hair. "I want more," she whispered.

"Well, that's a coincidence…"

"Bed, this time?"

"Bed is good."

"Carry me…"

"Yeah?"

"I have no bones, and that's your fault."

He laughed. It felt very, very good to make a woman boneless. "In that case, you're right, I need to carry you."

So he took her upstairs, and neither of them even thought about Kyle again that night.

Chapter Seven

Andy and Claudia drove up from New York City with Claudia's baby, Ben, on Wednesday evening, arriving at around seven and needing some help with unpacking the alarming amount of baby gear.

Their presence next door changed everything, of course.

It forced Scarlett to think, and to confront what she and Daniel were doing.

Which was, basically, spending a lot of time together in bed. Or on the couch. Or up against the kitchen wall. Or even on a blanket under a thick-leaved oak tree in the back garden, with the side gate locked and nighttime darkness providing a safe shield.

A lot of time in bed, and not much else.

Even though Andy technically lived next door, he and Claudia were under the same roof as Scarlett, sharing the same hot water system, the same garden, the same front porch.

This was how he and Claudia had met, in fact. She had

been a single-by-choice mom-to-be, renting this apartment on a short-term lease so that her baby could be born in a relaxed setting and so that both of them would come home from the rural Vermont hospital, after the birth, to a quiet routine.

She hadn't expected to find a daddy for her baby right on her doorstep, but it had happened and she and Andy were both blissfully happy about it. Now, instead of returning permanently to the city, the two of them were attempting a temporary long-distance relationship while she explored the idea of setting up her own accountancy and financial planning business here in Vermont.

All of which was great. Scarlett liked Claudia more every time they met, and it was gorgeous to see Andy learning how to become a dad to adorable little Ben.

But Ben cried a lot—Claudia had become much more laid-back about it lately, she said, and he was getting more settled now—and Scarlett and Daniel couldn't exactly fail to notice when the baby, his mom and his new dad were around. Scarlett didn't know how much she wanted her brother to notice in return.

For example, on Thursday morning when Daniel stayed for breakfast, it must have been very obvious that his car had been parked in her driveway all night. She tried to put her discomfort into words to Daniel, but they were clumsy ones, inadequate and hesitant and lacking in logic or sense. Even to her own ears they sounded wrong, out loud. "I feel exposed. Under a microscope."

"We're consenting adults, Scarlett," Daniel said, spilling a drop of milk from his cereal onto a very bare chest, because breakfast was happening in bed, along with this conversation. He didn't notice the bead of white liquid, too busy searching for the right way to make his point. "We're not cheating. We're not stripping off in plain sight. Is it really a problem? Why is it a problem? I'm not ashamed of a single thing about it."

But she couldn't explain.

There was a whole mess of different feelings and reactions inside her, and she couldn't explain any of them. He looked good in her bed. Sexy and lazy and *right*. She felt almost drunk from the touch of him, waterlogged with lovemaking, as if she'd spent hours in a river or a pool on a summer's day.

She told herself it was just sex, but there was no "just" about it. It was meaningful, delicious, important, perfect sex. Sex that changed everything. Sex that made possibilities and problems and questions she'd never thought about before.

Having Andy next door made her confront the raft of contradictions and impossibilities. The thought of dissecting and analyzing their relationship the way Kyle had always forced her to do during their marriage and their divorce almost brought on nausea.

The physical connection between her and Daniel was so powerful it shook her to the depths of her being, but what did that mean? What happened when it burned itself out? Would it burn itself out? What would be left?

Sex made her vulnerable.

This was about the only thing she was completely clear on.

Making love to Daniel with such need and such electric heat made her vulnerable and exposed, and if she had no choice about exposing herself to his power over her emotions, then at least she didn't have to expose herself to Andy and Claudia at the same time.

She didn't have to be so aware of them.

Knowing.

Talking.

Wondering.

She put her half-empty mug of coffee down on the bed-side table and launched herself across the rumpled sheets to Daniel. He lay there, propped up by two thick pillows, his empty cereal bowl on the other bedside table and that droplet of milk still only partly dried on his bare chest. She licked it off, tasting the faint, warm sweetness mingled with the salt from his skin, deliberately leaning over him, wondering inside, in a slightly panicky way, when she'd grown to be such a tease and why she needed it.

She scared herself. *Terrified* herself.

"What's this about?" he asked her, in a voice that was half growl, half honey.

"You spilled some milk. I got rid of it."

"I'm sensing there's something else, but your little blue nightdress is way too distracting. I swear it doesn't even reach the tops of your thighs, and those straps are the thickness of dental floss, and that little bra-top type thing on the inside coupled with the dippy neckline is…"

He never finished.

Started something else instead, and finished *that* with enormous thoroughness and shared satisfaction.

And it didn't solve a thing.

"Can we go to your place tonight?" she asked afterward, as they both clung to the last precious moments before he had to put on his uniform and she had to dress down in her woodworking clothes for a day in Aaron's workshop.

She could feel his muscles tense around her as they lay sprawled on the messy bed. "Because of Andy and Claudia and Ben next door?"

"Does there have to be a reason?" she answered. "We've spent all our time here, not there. Okay, yes, because of them."

"You've been passing my place on your way back and forth. Are you sure you want to spend time there?"

"I haven't even worked out which one it is. I know which one I hope it is. And I really hope you don't have a secret life as a fan of huge groupings of plastic flowers, or as someone called Sue who is the proprietor of a home hair salon."

"Sue is a great lady and a good neighbor. She cuts my hair. I can give you her phone number if you like. The plastic flowers are a slightly different story, but Eileen is a nice lady, too, and whatever floats her boat…"

"Daniel…"

"It's the one with the cars, okay?" he said, and his muscles tightened more.

"Hey, I was right!"

"You were *hoping* it was the house with the cars?" He pushed away a little, and propped himself up on one elbow.

"They look interesting. There must be some classic models, there." She reached for him, not wanting the distance that he'd tried to create. She rested her hand across his stomach, loving the hard, flat shapes of his muscles, but they weren't relaxed the way she wanted them.

"They don't look interesting when you've been living in their shadows for nearly thirty years," he said. His face was frowning and tight, his lips pressing together as if he'd said all he wanted.

It wasn't enough. "Tell me," she whispered. "Please?"

"Oh, hell, Scarlett…"

"Try. Make me understand."

"Watching them pile up and start to rust."

"Cars do that."

"And nothing ever was done with them. They were my dad's. He spent years accumulating them, more and more, spending money we didn't have, taking up the space where there used to be grass and trees, hauling in half-wrecked sheds to put a roof over them if he thought they might have value. Even when they were free, or even if he got a little money to take them, my mother struggled with them. He always had these huge, vague plans for them. Restoring them. Starting a museum. Dealing in parts. But then he left and never came back for them." Another silent struggle, between speech and silence. "And then he died when I was in my teens."

There was a lot edited out, Scarlett could tell. Edited out for *her,* or was it just the way he was? "And yet they're still there," she said.

"Not for much longer. Look, I know they don't send a great message." He shifted fully away from her and rolled off the bed before she could pull him back. He went hunting for his jeans and all she could do was watch.

"It's not a problem," she said. "I told you. They're interesting."

But he was intent on his own explanation. He held the jeans in front of his naked body, without putting them on. "None of it's going to be there much longer. My sister is coming next week, I think I told you, and we're going to go through the whole house and sheds and yard, sort out the stuff, get the place ready to sell. We needed a little time before we tackled it." He cleared his throat and blinked a few times, reminding her that his mother's death was still fresh, even though her illness hadn't been.

"Of course you did."

"I need to talk to Paula and Jordan about what they want, do some research to see if anyone wants the cars. Mom was too ill for us to do much about it, by the time my dad died. She needed everything quiet. She didn't need the distress. We talked about it a few times, but she always ended up saying, no, she couldn't face it, could we leave them awhile longer."

"I can see that. It would have been horrible if you'd had people and tow trucks and heavy vehicles coming and going." She slid reluctantly from the bed. Daniel had put on his jeans. It was time for her to get dressed, also.

"And then my sister couldn't get away for enough of a block of time, until now." He found his shirt and held it scrunched in his hand.

"The house looked pretty and nice. I noticed the new deck." She opened a drawer.

"I put that on for Mom, in stages, so she had somewhere outside to sit. Even if the view mainly consisted of rusting metal."

"I want to come to your place tonight, Daniel. The cars are fine."

"They look worse close up." He was testing her, daring her, the way he had six years ago. Making it blunt and in her face. *Can you handle this, Scarlett? Or are you going to run a mile?*

And she had run a mile.

But not for the reasons he thought.

This time, she had to be braver. And stronger.

"I'm sure they do," she told him, grabbing the first bra and matching panties that she found. "I'm more concerned about the state of your bathroom, since you're male and living alone."

"My bathroom is decent," he growled, and dived into the shirt.

"There you go." She clipped up her bra.

He looked at her, and for once his focus wasn't the underwear. "You're trying to keep this light, Scarlett, but it's not working." His face showed the truth of the words.

There were lines of tension at the corners of his gorgeous mouth and his eyes seemed to glitter.

She kept it flippant. "Yeah, you picked up on that, too?"

"Hey…"

He seemed to want this serious, so she changed her tone. "This thing is still between us, Daniel, the fact that you think I can't handle your background."

"Isn't it why we broke up?" He took some restless paces through the room.

No.

It wasn't.

Not really.

Not at heart.

She knew it, but the thought of putting the knowledge into words scared her, because she didn't know what she would have to say about their breakup instead. There was so much more to it than what he'd said, but the truth was all a mess inside her and she didn't know how to sort the mess out. It cut both ways, too, she was sure. He wasn't sorted out inside himself, either.

What counted in a relationship? What made it last? What were the breaking points, and the things you couldn't get past?

"What was the reason, then?" he asked.

"It was only a part," she answered him. "Do you think the fact that I had a very comfortable childhood means there's nothing I doubt about my own life, and my own choices? Why would I ever have married a man like Kyle, if I had all the right priorities in place? Don't you think I have regrets and questions, too?"

"You want to talk about those?"

"No, not particularly. The same way you don't. Because it might scare me. It might scare us both."

"Tell me some of it."

She shrugged. "I'm scared of the disconnect between what I *think* and what I *feel*. Dad tells me this stuff about my brain and my capabilities and my obligations as a doctor, and I feel pushed into a box that's too tight and doesn't fit. I want to find a different way. I want different priorities. Or different compass points. Or something. But what should those compass points be? We don't need to cover it now, do we?"

"We can't cover it now," he said, reluctance slowing the words. "I have to go." They looked at each other, helpless and not connecting, with words or without them. "Do you want to meet at my place right after you finish with Aaron? I'll be home around five."

"Five sounds good."

"I'll pick up some dinner."

"I can bring wine."

They both heard Claudia come out into the backyard with Ben in her arms. He was fussing and she was cooing to him about the pretty birds and flowers, trying to get him to settle.

"I have to go," Daniel said again, and left the house less than two minutes later.

Scarlett took things more slowly, packing an overnight bag with a couple of clothing changes, but in twenty minutes, she was behind the wheel, too, on her way to Aaron and Judy's.

She stopped on the way for the bottle of wine she'd promised to bring to Daniel's tonight, then slowed on her way past the house with the yard full of cars, and looked at it with extra curiosity now she knew that it was definitely his, that the cars had belonged to his father, and that he hated them.

It was true, they were a mess. There were rows and heaps of them, some without wheels and piled on blocks, others in better shape and housed beneath the roofing of several broken-down sheds. She understood why they bothered him, but she still felt their upside-down attraction.

They were Daniel's.

They were a part of his past and his life.

Which made them important.

In Aaron's workshop, Judy greeted her with fresh-brewed coffee and a sweet, homemade treat as usual. "You're spoiling me," Scarlett told her.

"I love to bake, and I love good coffee." She held a large, bowl-shaped china cup in her hands, not by the handle but with her fingers pressed against the rim. Backing her words with action, she poised her face over the cup and inhaled deeply. "I think I love the smell even more than the taste."

"Me, too. It always smells so great here. Coffee and sugar and wood shavings. I love it."

"I said to Aaron yesterday, you look like a kid in a candy store each morning when your head peeks around that door."

"I know." She gave a shrug that was half an apology, half not. "Should I be embarrassed about that? I've never done anything like this before. I love being a doctor…I think I do…but it's so different. Even when my hands are involved, during a physical exam, it's not like this. It's clinical and dry. It's about science, not art and craft."

"There's science in this, too," Aaron said, a little defensively. "Measurement and chemistry and the physical properties of wood."

"There is," Scarlett had to agree. "You think I'm not traveling as far outside my comfort zone as I think?"

"I think you are," Judy said firmly. "And I think it's

wonderful that you're exploring such a different side to yourself."

And of course this made Scarlett think of Daniel, and what she was exploring with him.

He'd only just gotten home when she arrived at his place that afternoon. She saw him pause beside his vehicle with his keys in his hand and watch her approach. As she parked, he went up the steps to the deck, but then paused again, turned and came to meet her. He was still in his trooper's uniform, which fitted snug enough across his broad shoulders and chest to make his level of fitness and strength very clear.

"Wearing our work gear, both of us," she said, dropping her overnight bag on his deck and brushing her hands down her T-shirt and jeans in an attempt to remove the lingering pieces of wood dust and shavings.

"You smell like cedar, even from this distance. It's nice."

"It's stronger, closer up. I think it works very well in tandem with my shampoo..."

But he didn't respond to her tease and stayed where he was, standing with his feet braced and motionless and his arms held away from his sides, frowning. She realized that her own words had been too forced. They were both so self-conscious and awkward about the childhood home he'd never shown her six years ago, even though he'd brought her up here back then with that plan in mind.

"I'm so sorry that I never got to come here and meet your mom," she blurted out.

He just nodded in answer, and she felt it had been an inadequate thing to say. Sincere but empty, and she didn't know where to go next.

"Show me around," she said, sweeping her arm around

to show that she didn't mean his kitchen, bedroom and bath. She didn't want to go inside yet.

In case they just ended up in bed? Would that be such a problem?

Something told her it would, today. Today, and here, the place he'd been raised. There were other things to deal with, first. They had something to prove to each other about the strength of their connection, and they couldn't prove it with bed.

And there were the cars.

"You really want to?" he drawled, as if he didn't believe her.

"Yes, I really want to." She wasn't the only one with issues about awkwardness and inadequacy. "Show me the cars."

"The cars."

"Yes. Please. Show me where your property boundary is. Looks as if you have a couple of acres, at least."

"Four acres."

"That's a decent piece of land."

"I'm going to sell it," he reminded her. "It's owned three ways, from Mom's will. My sister, Paula, my brother, Jordan, and me. It belonged to Mom's parents, originally."

"You've barely said anything about your brother. He's not local anymore, right?"

"He's still in college. Medical school, actually."

"Wow, that's great. You didn't tell me."

"There's a lot we haven't told each other yet, don't you think?" he said on a growl.

"Listen, if he ever needs any help. When he's ready to choose a specialty… Anything."

"Thanks. He has another couple of years to go, so no decisions to make yet."

They still weren't connecting. There were so many

questions she wanted to ask, so many things she sensed he wasn't saying, and there was a barrier clearly in place. It read Keep Out. She didn't know whether to be angry with him, or to bleed for him. She didn't know in any detail what there was to bleed *about*.

"Show me the cars," she repeated.

He looked at her, with a searching, suffering expression on his face. "You're serious, aren't you?"

She took a breath. "Of course I'm serious." Because she could see that the cars were important.

He controlled a sigh. "Okay, you asked for it."

"Yeah, I did."

So he took her on a tour of the erratic pathways that ran between the rusty heaps and rows, and she discovered he'd barely looked at the cars himself. It had to be a deliberate closing off, to have stayed away from them for this long.

To have refused to even *see* them, almost.

Now, he was playing the polite host, leading her past wreck after wreck. There had to be a hundred cars here. More. Some had grass growing up through their rusted-out interiors. Some looked at her through the blind eyes of missing windshields. Daniel had his face set so hard, Scarlett thought it might crack. She wanted to take his arm, turn this into a casual stroll, but it wasn't going to happen.

Not yet.

"Sheesh, this is a DeSoto from the fifties," Daniel muttered at one point, as they stood side by side, staring into the run-down three-walled shed. "And this is a Dodge Wayfarer. When did they stop making those?"

She asked him carefully, "You didn't know they were here? After all this time?"

The Keep Out sign was back in place. If it had ever

been taken down. "I've had better things to do than come out here, taking inventory."

"Your whole life?"

"Scarlett, I don't want to talk about this." He looked like a rock, standing there, staring at the cars, his shoulders hunched and his forearms wrapped around each other, across the front of his chest.

She touched his warm arm, touched the tensed, bulging shape of his muscle, aching for the barrier and what might be behind it. "Yeah, really? You don't?" she said gently. "Gee, I hadn't picked up on that."

"So why are you pushing?"

Because sex isn't everything.

Because sex isn't *anything* if there's *only* sex.

Wasn't that true?

The question kept hitting her and scaring her, confronting her in and out of bed, and she didn't have the answer. Didn't they need a whole lot more than sex, if this relationship was going to be real, in any way?

"Because I think we need to talk about this."

"Yeah?"

"I think you've never truly looked at your own yard. I think you see it in your head as way worse than it is. I want you to look, Daniel. I want you to see something different."

"Something different."

"Something good. Which is what I see."

He didn't reply.

They stood. They stared at the cars. There were twisted hoods and empty windows, fallen bumpers and perished tires, stretches of original paint, glimpses of intact detail and engine parts, and there was rust, rust, rust.

But the cars were beautiful. They were. As beautiful in their way as Aaron's wood in all its different stages of treatment and completion. They had luscious curved shapes and accidental patterns in their rust patches, and they had secret history. They had *potential*.

Daniel unfolded his arms and wiped the back of his neck with the palm of his hand. He looked a little less tight, a little less angry. Bewildered, in some way. Wrestling with all sorts of things. He kicked at a flattened tire and ran his hand over the curve of a side mirror.

Looking.

Thinking.

Facing his demons.

In the quiet between them, Scarlett found some hope, and the courage to go slow. She stepped a little closer and took his arm, which meant that her cheek could pillow itself just at his shoulder. He could have detached himself from the contact, but he didn't, he just stayed still and silent, looking at the cars.

"I like this old lady," Scarlett said. She prodded her toe against the rusty grille of a brave old tank of a thing that still managed to show off much of its once glorious red paint on each side.

"She's a girl, that one?" Daniel's voice sounded almost as rusty as the machines.

"Because of her rouged cheeks."

"What about that one?" He nodded his head at a 1970s Ford, resting drunkenly in the back corner of the shed with one door hanging open.

"Definitely male. And not the kind you'd take to meet your grandmother, with all that chrome and black paint. Classic bad boy."

Daniel laughed and looked at her. "You have too much imagination." He pulled her into his arms suddenly, and she went, because it felt good there, no matter what else was happening.

He buried his face in her hair and breathed in the scent that she barely smelled now after living with it all day— the fresh wood. He didn't speak. She wanted him to at first, because of all the unsaid things, but then it started to seem as if silence was better.

As long as they were holding each other. As long as the tension and anger and blocking weren't there. She tried to say everything with her body.

I'm here. I want you. I trust this. I trust who you are, and where you came from. Talk to me.

Could she say that much without any words?

He muttered something under his breath that she didn't catch, then spoke her name. "It's okay," she whispered back, even though she didn't know if it was. Not really. They stood without moving, and finally Daniel began to speak.

"He used to take me with him," he said. "Starting from when I was maybe eight or nine. I hated it. He had a tow truck. It barely ran. He would have been drinking. We'd go and collect some wreck. He'd haggle over the price. Sometimes he'd get paid to take the wreck away, sometimes he'd pay, if he thought the car was worth something. He'd tell the guy—whoever it was—that this was our project, his and mine, that we were going to restore the cars, salvage the parts. At first I believed him. I used to say to him on a weekend, 'Can we get to work on the cars today, Dad?' I really thought it was our project and that it was going to happen, that I'd end up with a shiny, beautiful car that would be mine. You know, I was the eldest son, the eldest child, I wanted that connection with Dad, the man-to-man thing. We went to car shows a couple of times, and I thought one day that would be me and Dad, showing off our '57 Chevy, all pimped up. Maybe a few times we did start on something, but he always had a beer in his hand at the same time, and the first roadblock we hit—like he didn't have the right tool, or something he needed was broken or missing—he'd stop and curse and go back in the house for more beer and TV. By the time I was ten or eleven, I knew nothing was ever going to happen. I tried to do some work on them myself, but he got mad at that, he wouldn't let me, said I didn't know anything—but then he wouldn't teach me—and by then my mom was getting sick. So that was it for the cars." He fell silent.

That was it for his relationship with his dad, too, Scarlett guessed, and the cars were an ever-present symbol, which he couldn't evade or move because he'd had to take care of his mom.

"What was it, your mom's illness?" she asked.

"Lupus. She had the rash across her face, kidney problems, heart problems. She had everything. She couldn't tolerate the sun. She only sat on the deck after sunset."

"Who took care of her, the years you were in New York?"

"My sister, and my brother. But then Jordan hit college age, and he was bright so Paula and I decided we needed to make college possible for him, and she got married around then, too, and her husband's job took him to Boston. That was when I came back here, to take over."

"She was a good person, your mom."

"She was a great person. She didn't deserve—" He stopped.

"No. Of course she didn't. Any of it."

They stood there in silence once more. She held him, barely daring to move, hoping the warmth and press of her body was enough. Hoping it was right, that it said the right things.

He kissed the top of her head, pressing his mouth there with a slow heat that she could feel like a brand. She let the kisses come, nuzzling her face into the hardness between his collarbone, breathing him in.

Soon it wasn't enough. She turned her face up, wanting the kiss closer and deeper. Impatience surged in her.

Please. Now. I want to feel you and taste you, cement this connection we managed to make with our words.

He bent his head, seeking the same thing, even more impatient than she was, after those long moments of stillness and silence. Their cheeks crushed together. She felt clumsy about it, as if it wasn't possible to get close enough without a little mess first. A bump on her jaw. Her mouth landing against his chin and the corners of his lips instead of where she wanted it.

Finally they connected, the contact moist and full and naked. *Just kiss me. Just keep my mouth on yours. Just touch me. Wherever you want. For as long as you want.*

She felt as if her body belonged totally to him, and his body to her, and the sense of shared ownership was so scary and new. *Could* you own someone else's body? Could they own you? In a good way? Or was it damaging and destructive to feel this strongly?

To feel this about every inch of his skin. About every taste, and every movement.

She was shaking within a few minutes, and the kiss didn't end. They stood there with the cars watching them through their blind, empty eyes, and they could so easily have lain down on the grass, screened from human sight by the rows and heaps of wreckage and made love then and there.

Except that this almost went beyond sex. If they made love right now, it would eventually peak and ebb, and they'd have to pull apart. If they just kept holding each other, touching each other, they didn't need to think about what came next.

Just kiss me. Just hold me. Just say my name.

But at some point it had to happen.

Nothing like this could last, unless the world itself stopped. Today, the world refused to cooperate, and went right on turning. It was getting late.

"Save the rest for later?" Daniel muttered. The light had perceptibly changed, moving toward evening. It must be six o'clock, at least.

"If I still have legs."

"I'll carry you. I can do that, remember? I carried you from your car, by the side of the road. I carried you to your bedroom. Twice."

"Don't carry me. But don't let me go."

They made their way back to the house, between the piles of cars, whose power over him she understood, now. They were such a physical symbol and reminder. They weren't easy to ignore, and his attempt to ignore them, to forget what was there, had only made their power stronger.

Chapter Eight

"I bought steaks," Daniel said as they neared the steps going up to the deck. "They're still in the trunk of the car, along with some other stuff for a barbecue. I saw you turn into the yard and forgot all about them."

"Steak sounds good."

He opened up the trunk and she helped him carry four or five shopping bags up the steps. "Enough for a week, Daniel."

"The thing is, I may have a guest staying some nights." He smiled at her sideways, a little sheepish and teasing at the same time. "I wasn't sure what she liked, so I got everything."

Everything included potatoes and sour cream and salad fixings, breakfast cereal, two brands of coffee, two kinds of milk, three kinds of bread, paper towel and ice cream and fruit and soap that smelled of lavender... The list went on, and she loved what it said about his thoughtfulness.

He'd shopped for her last week, too, and on the weekend. He'd helped her set up her apartment.

She loved what these actions said about him, on top of the flow of words he'd unleashed just now.

He set up the homemade barbecue on the back deck, opened out some folding chairs. He uncorked the bottle of red wine she'd brought, and wrapped potatoes in foil to place in the heap of coals he made in the depths of the half drum of the barbecue. Meanwhile, Scarlett made the salad and found dressing for it in the refrigerator, as well as plates and glasses and silverware.

All action. Not much talk at all. It felt peaceful and un-hurried and nice, and she decided not to question it, but to trust it instead. Maybe she tied herself up too much with questioning and logic, didn't go enough with her gut, didn't find the right things to trust.

When the potatoes were done, Daniel used tongs to pull them from the coals, and set them on the grill to keep warm, while he tossed on the steaks, poured a splash of wine on them for flavor and stood back as they sizzled and hissed. The smell almost made Scarlett's tongue sting, it was so good.

She went inside to bring out the salad and paused for a while to take in the details of the house. The rooms were cozy in size and paneled in a warm, syrupy pine. The fur-niture was plain and basic, two matching couches with squishy upholstery and blue fabric. There were family photos and several handmade quilts on the walls, with fabric colors and patterns that suggested they'd been handed down through the family for two or three genera-tions.

Daniel found her studying them and told her, "My great-grandmother and my grandmother made those. Mom was never as good with a needle, but she repaired the seams when they split. They used to be folded away in a closet, but then we decided it was crazy not to have them out to look at, so we put them up."

"They look beautiful."

"They're pretty faded and worn, some of 'em."

"I like that they're not perfect. I love that about old things—the cars, too—that their history shows."

"Steaks are almost done," Daniel told her. "I need to turn them."

"I'll be out in a minute...if you don't mind me looking some more, at the quilts and the photos."

"Of course I don't mind."

So she browsed the photos, finding Daniel as an urchin of a child with his sister and brother, his mom with some older relatives, his dad as a vigorous young man holding up a freshly caught fish and standing proudly beside a shiny 1970s Ford with a beer in his hand.

Daniel's family. Daniel's history. It was messy and imperfect and bittersweet, but it belonged to him and him alone, it had formed him and so it was precious to her.

He called out to her, "Better come eat while they're still sizzling."

She went, with the feeling that her emotions had been stirred to their depths.

The sun began to sink behind the hill as they ate, softening the summer heat and light. Daniel had lit mosquito coils and citronella candles, which, along with the drifts of smoke from the dying barbecue, were enough to keep biting creatures away.

The wine was mellow and rich in Scarlett's mouth. The lengthening shadows made the light so beautiful, and the cars looked like sleeping creatures in their cloaks of mottled color.

Why did anyone need to speak?

The peacefulness of the silence spoke for them. Scarlett let her mind drift to the hospital, to the endless phone consults and meetings with colleagues, the often emotional conferences with parents, the back and forth with nurses over tests ordered, tests back, results given.

She knew she needed a better balance. Her home life couldn't just be a gasp of desperate breath before she plunged back into the stormy sea. Maybe she needed to take inspiration from Andy and leave New York. She needed to accept that she wasn't the kind of person who could switch on and off at will, which meant she needed a less stressful work environment, and easier avenues of escape.

Dad always thought that was somehow a sign of weakness, but didn't it strengthen you, to understand and accept the person you were, with all your assets and all your limitations? Why live in denial?

And why put pressure on herself to make all her decisions and answer all her questions less than two weeks into her time away?

She realized that Daniel was watching her, sitting back in his chair with his legs stretched out and crossed at the ankles, and his fingers laced behind his head. She waited for him to ask what she was thinking, or come out with something about the direction of his own thoughts, but he didn't.

Just smiled, and said, "So nice."

"It's great."

They sat some more, and she felt her way deeper into the silence. There were crickets chirping and the fireflies had come out, their lights winking on, hovering, and winking off again. A car went by on the road, the *whooshing* sound cool and pleasant from this distance.

She looked at Daniel and found his gaze on her once

again, and this time neither of them said a word, and even his slow, lazy smile—just his *smile,* for heck's sake, at a distance of at least eight feet!—made her want to rip off his clothes and jump his bones and wake up still holding him in the morning.

And somehow he knew that.

He just stood up, still without a word, and held out his hand for her, and she went, and it was heaven.

Daniel didn't know what had woken him. A car going by outside. An animal noise in the night. Whatever it was, he went from deep sleep to blinking wakefulness in the space of seconds and found Scarlett beside him, breathing slow and steady, with her sweetly naked back curved against his chest, and her bottom nestled into his groin.

He didn't want to wake her....

Or maybe he did.

A part of him definitely did.

He resisted, and tried to school himself into sleep again.

That never worked. There were shadows in the room, and there was too much light coming from outside. He realized he'd left the outdoor lights on, from when they'd sat on the deck eating their meal. It didn't matter. It wasn't important. But it nagged at him all the same.

Then he heard another noise.

Raccoons. Could even be a black bear.

He and Scarlett hadn't cleared away the remnants of their meal. They'd had other things on their minds. He eased himself away from her delicious body—she'd definitely started putting back the extra weight she needed—and rolled out of the bed, groping for the pajama bottoms he'd left scrunched beneath his pillow.

Out in the living area, he saw the light spilling in from the deck and then a moving shadow accompanied by the sound of a clatter and scampering feet. Definitely raccoons. He went out and found the T-bones from the steak littered on the wood, as well as some leafy remnants of salad.

The raccoons had disappeared. They had a hundred possible sheltering places out in his yard. He looked.

There was a moon out. It shone on the wrecks, stripping out the colors of paint and rust and leaving only a gray scale with touches of silver everywhere, in the reflections from glass and chrome, in the metallic finish of the 1970s muscle cars.

Scarlett was right, he realized. There was a strange kind of beauty to it all. There was potential and promise. Car buffs would consider the place a treasure trove. If he could get the word out, he might actually make people *happy* about all these hulking, shadowy shapes. Over the years, even though this was a quiet back road, he—or Paula, or Jordan, or Mom—had gotten the occasional visitor at his door, or a message left in his mailbox.

"I was passing by. Are these vehicles for sale? Please call me."

But he'd never called the numbers scribbled in the messages, and he'd turned the visitors away. Mom, Paula and Jordan had done the same thing.

Different reasons, maybe.

His own reasons he understood a little better after that flood of words to Scarlett. Shoot, how long since he'd talked like that, all in one hit? He couldn't even think. And he hadn't given her any choice but to listen.

It wasn't just about the stress on Mom. He'd been punishing his long-gone father with those cars. Punishing himself, too. Punishing his childhood self for the naïveté of believing in a man who couldn't change.

Crazy.

Dumb.

Over.

Move on, Daniel. Because you're not Dad. You won't let it happen. You can *change.*

He picked up the leftover mess from dinner, piled up plates and silverware and barbecue tongs, dumped it all in the kitchen sink and shut the lights on the deck. The raccoons would probably prefer it that way, but they wouldn't find the pickings as rich now. They could go eat berries in the woods instead.

His feet and shoulders were chilly. He went back to the bedroom and found Scarlett awake and looking at him. "What happened?"

"Raccoons. We didn't clear up."

"We had other priorities."

He slid into the bed, and remembered where his thoughts had been before the distraction of the animal noise outside. "What are your priorities now?"

"Ow, first, warming your feet," she said. "*Ow,* and your hands!"

"How're we going to manage that?"

"I have a couple of ideas…"

They stayed awake for another hour, and then they almost slept late.

Chapter Nine

Daniel wasn't sure if there were rules about dating and puppies.

He thought there probably were.

You probably weren't supposed to bring a woman along with you to choose a puppy until you had half your clothes at each other's houses, had exchanged anecdotes about the worst thing that ever happened to you at school and knew each other's top three favorite movies, foods and bands.

He decided he didn't care. He and Scarlett had agreed not to see each other on Friday night, but at eight o'clock that evening when his friends Greg and Lena called to confirm that he could pick up his pup this weekend, he knew he wanted to bring her along.

Greg and Lena bred Labradors, and he'd told them several months ago that he wanted to have one from their bitch Molly's next litter. The desire for a dog had been nagging at him for a long time, but there was always too much getting in the way, too many reasons why it wasn't a good idea. But the wheel of life had shifted after Mom's death in February, and with the first flush of spring back in late March had come the realization that at last the time was right.

Molly had produced seven pups. He'd met them when they were just a tangle of paws and ears, and permanently attached to their mother's side, but he hadn't wanted to make his choice when they were still so small. Now they were just over eight weeks old, which was the perfect time.

Greg and Lena had promised him first pick of the litter. "So it would be really great if you could come tomorrow morning," Lena reminded him on the phone, "because we have four more people wanting to take theirs this weekend, too."

"Tomorrow morning for sure, then," he told her, then added before he could stop himself—not to mention before he knew if Scarlett would even want to come—"Is it okay if I bring a friend?"

"Of course!" He could hear her struggling not to ask what *kind* of a friend.

"It might just be me," he had to say. "I need to check if she's available."

"Hope she is," Lena answered lightly, and he managed to end the call before she lost her inner battle and pushed him for details.

He called Scarlett at once, knowing he was in serious danger of second-guessing himself and chickening out of the whole idea, and when she said, "Wow, a puppy! I've never had a dog. Wow! I would *love* to help you choose…" he had to fight not to pump his fist in the air.

"That's great," he said.

Then he heard her add, "If you think I'll be the slightest bit of help, when I have no expertise."

"Doesn't take expertise. Just takes eyes and heart."

"Good."

He picked her up at nine, when the late summer air was still cool and the shadows long.

"I didn't know what to wear," she said, coming out of the house, "but looks as if I was right with the dress code." They were both wearing jeans and casual T-shirts, hers in a pattern of pink with tiny silver beads scattered here and there.

"Yeah, it could get messy," he agreed, as they both climbed into his car.

"What breed?"

"Labrador."

"What color?"

"Black."

"Oh, how gorgeous! This is such a new experience." She laughed. "I—I seriously can't remember when I've ever seen puppies so young. Never. Will it be a boy or a girl?"

"Don't know."

"How will you decide?"

"I'm thinking that we'll sit and look and play and take our time… Do you have time?" He looked across at her.

She had her seat belt fastened, her butt a little crooked so that her shoulder rested against the window, and her legs kicked loosely out in front of her. She looked happy to be here, happy to be with him, happy about the puppy, and every molecule of air inside the vehicle seemed to hum with their sense of each other.

His heart lifted, it was crazy. This puffy, bubbly feeling inside him made it hard to even breathe.

"I have all day," she said. "I have family coming up from the city, but they won't get here until late afternoon."

"So we have until late afternoon?"

"If you want."

"Oh, I want." Shoot, he couldn't drive, yet. It wouldn't be safe.

They just sat there, looking at each other, smiling goofily, not wanting to break the moment with words.

Or even with movement.

Finally she gave a sigh that seemed to contain the same light, bubbly happiness he felt himself. "I'm so glad you asked me to do this with you, Daniel."

"Me, too," he confessed gruffly. "Almost didn't."

"Why?"

"Wasn't sure of the rules. Dating and puppies. You know?"

"The rule that a puppy is code for 'let's take this to the next level'?" she said.

"Yeah, that rule."

"Let's not have rules."

"Suits me."

"Let's make up our own rules, and change them whenever we want," she said, smiling at him. Not a huge smile, just a small, teasing one that came and went on her mouth and made it impossible for him to look away.

"Let's keep them to a list of ten or less," he managed to say.

"Let's definitely do that. And there aren't going to be any levels."

"You don't like levels? You put a lot of scathing into that word."

"Levels are like rules. Prescriptive. I'm trying to get over being prescriptive, having my life governed by things I *should* want, and *should* do, and *should* think and feel."

"Agreed. Sounds healthy."

"Feels healthy, so far."

"The rules we do have, will we write them down?"

"Nope."

"Could get set in stone, that way, and we don't want that."

"No, we don't," she agreed. Damn that smile!

He pressed his lips together, looked away at last. Okay, maybe *now* he could manage to drive. He started the engine, put the car into gear and didn't immediately crash into a mailbox or a garden wall.

Which was a positive sign.

"Tell me more about the puppy," Scarlett said as they reached the outskirts of town. "What are our search criteria?"

"Well, I've been thinking I probably want the quietest one in the litter."

"Yeah?"

"Labradors are pretty energetic, and I won't be home enough to keep a really demanding personality under control. I'll need one that's more laid-back."

"Laid-back. Got it."

"But I'm open to gut feelings, too. I kind of feel it just has to hit us which one is right. You said it before—I don't want to go with *should,* either."

"Even with a puppy."

"Even with a puppy."

It was a half-hour drive to Greg and Lena's. They didn't talk much, after that riff on rules and stuff. Scarlett said at one point, "Vermont is so pretty," and that was about it. Daniel found the silence quite satisfactory, personally, but it bothered him a little that she might not feel the same. Weren't you supposed to talk a mile a minute in a situation like this? Spill every detail? Discover a thousand things in common every time you opened your mouth?

He hated the pressure to decorate every social interaction with a wallpaper of words. He couldn't. He didn't trust the kinds of things you thought you were learning about a person during such conversations, anyhow. Actions said more than words.

Okay, so that was hokey, that had been said a million times before, but it was still true. His download to her on Thursday he didn't regret, he felt healed by it, good about it, but it wasn't something he wanted to repeat every week.

Finally, just before they arrived, Scarlett said to him, "Can I say something silly?"

"No, that's banned. Rule five. Surely you knew." But then he glanced at her and saw that she looked timid and serious, and he realized it was something important, so he added quickly, "Hey, of course…" He would have pulled her into his arms if he hadn't been driving.

"I really and seriously don't know anything about dogs. My parents thought it wasn't fair to have one in a city apartment, and of course they had a point. We had a cockatiel."

"Slightly different."

"Just slightly. And as an adult I've had no pets at all. I know puppies are cute. I mean, how could I not? But is there any protocol? Could I really mess up with this? With your friends?"

He slowed the car and looked at her, sitting there with a little frown and tensed shoulders. "You're not going to mess up. How? We're just going to look, and play."

"Will they…um…pee on me?"

"They shouldn't. Greg and Lena will have started housebreaking 'em. There might be a ways to go with that. I'll have to follow their method, and be consistent, once I have the dog at home. But you can usually tell when peeing is about to happen, and they'll have a box they're learning to use."

"Okay, that's a big question answered. I mean, I wore

old jeans, but not *that* old." She brushed her hands across her thighs, fingers fluttering a little.

"Hey, you really are nervous about this."

"Told you it was new." Her smile this time was tentative and apologetic, and he liked it just as much as the teasing one.

"You're going to be fine," he said, and leaned across the car to put his arm around her, steering with one hand. "Trust yourself. Stop overthinking." She nodded and pressed her lips together and he had to laugh. "Make sure you think very hard about the nonthinking bit, won't you?"

"Yeah, thanks for that..." But she was laughing, too.

At Greg and Lena's, seven puppies awaited them, in an extended and very doggy wing of the sprawling ranch-style house. The wing with its attached open-air runs had been built especially, when their breeding of Labradors grew from a hobby to a part-time business.

"You're staying for coffee, right?" Lena asked, after she'd ushered them into the puppies' play area.

"If you have time, guys."

"Of course we have time, Dan."

"Scarlett, coffee, too, if that's okay?" He looked at her, wanting to read her face, wondering if he could trust his gut on this one.

"Sounds great," she said, as if she meant it, and then there was a little back and forth between all four of them about how Scarlett took her coffee, and where they'd sit, and how long they wanted to spend with the puppies first.

Daniel didn't miss the little zing of unspoken assessment that passed back and forth during all this. It made him tense, but there wasn't a lot he could do about it. Of course his friends were going to be curious about who he'd brought. Of course Scarlett was going to wonder if she was being given points or a blackball for how she came across.

Puppies were less judgmental.

Puppies were a relief.

All seven of them were in a round blue plastic wading pool, tumbling over each other as they played and fought. He dropped to their level, made the right noises, picked up a ball, and two of them came across to him and started sniffing and exploring, their legs still seeming too long and floppy for their bodies.

Scarlett sat down, too. She was laughing. "They're so cute. They're *so cute.* I have no idea how you're even going to tell which one is which."

But in only a few minutes, the puppy personalities started to emerge. You could have named them like the dwarves in Snow White. The four boys Goofy, Reckless, Sleepy and Squealer, and the three girls Needy, Tomboy and Zany.

"I probably should pick the sleepy one," Daniel said. "According to what I told you in the car."

"Except maybe he's tired himself out being the most energetic and demanding dog in the universe until three minutes before you got here."

"You could be right."

"I'm feeling that your heart doesn't belong to the sleepy one."

"I'm not listening to my heart till I know if it's talking sense, but I'm going on the theory that it *probably* is."

"I like your planning, there."

There was the possibility of some deeper meaning to all of that, but they didn't go there. If it stayed in her mind, he wasn't going to know.

They played some more. Scarlett scooped up the goofy one and laughed as his legs wouldn't cooperate with his desperate desire to lick her face. Reckless fell over while trying to go after the ball. Tomboy was convinced she could balance on the rim of the wading pool, but she was wrong. Squealer thought this whole morning was so exciting that he had to be taken over to the special bathroom box twice in the space of ten minutes.

Scarlett was behaving like a three-year-old and refusing to share. She still had Goofy in her lap. "He's gone to sleep, what can I do?"

Lena opened the door and poked her head into the room to tell them that coffee was ready. "Is there a decision yet? Greg and I know which one we think you'll go for."

"I can't go for the one I want to go for, because Scarlett won't let him out of her lap."

"Not my fault," Scarlett said. "It just happened."

"Oh, that *is* the one you want? Percy?"

"You mean that's the one you had pegged? The goofy one?"

"Greg had him pegged for you. I wasn't so sure. Until the day he fell asleep *across* the rim of the wading pool with his legs not even touching the ground, and we could almost hear how you would have laughed."

"Percy's a cute name," Scarlett said.

"We always name them," Lena told her. "But a lot of people have their own ideas, and change the names we've given. They're not set in stone."

"I won't change it," Daniel said, and knew he'd given a little too much away about his feelings. And not his feelings about the dog. Bringing Scarlett, then keeping the name Percy just because she thought it was cute?

Yeah, Lena was pretty perceptive. She had a look on her face that said her unspoken questions on the phone last night had answers, now. Out loud, she kept it neutral and light, thank heaven. "Want to leave him while we have our coffee?"

"Will we really be able to pick him out of the litter

again, if we let him go?" Scarlett asked. "Maybe they'll all start to look alike, again, the way they did at first."

Lena laughed. "Trust me, we can always pick Percy."

They sat outside in a paved area beneath the trees. Lena had whipped up a batch of chocolate chip cookies, which were still warm and melty from the oven, and Greg looked very content with his marital status as he crumbled one into his mouth and stretched his long legs out in front of him.

"Are we rationed with these, hon?" He grabbed his red-headed wife as she went past and gave her a waist-height hug, his arm not stretching nearly as far around her as it had a few months ago. She was five or six months pregnant, with a baby they'd both been wanting and trying for, for a while.

Which kind of put Daniel's happiness about puppies-and-dating rules into perspective, and made him feel a long way behind the curve. You got to a point in life where you wanted what your friends had, in certain important areas, and you wondered what would happen to the friendship, and to yourself, if you didn't find them.

"Guests aren't rationed," Lena was saying to the father of her unborn child. "You are. Ration of two."

"Two?" Greg made an indignant grab for the plate and the cookies almost went flying.

Scarlett jumped up and took the plate from Lena as if it was a football and they were doing a linebacker passing drill. Lena said, "See, Scarlett, you earned three extra cookies just with that move." She gestured to the basketball hoop on the adjacent garage wall. "Any cookie you can make a basket with, you can have."

"Can I be a part of that arrangement?" Daniel asked.

Lena cast him a shrewd look. "Don't I recall that you played division-one high school basketball, at one time?"

"I forget. Did I?"

"Excuse me, let me just make my shot before the whole hoop is encrusted with chocolate and crumbs from someone else's efforts," Scarlett said.

"You're really going to do it." Greg was laughing.

"She is," said Lena. "Daniel, you're not."

"I think there is some kind of female, chocolate-related conspiracy going on here."

Scarlett stood beneath the hoop. "Who gets to eat this if I miss?"

"Depends if it hits the ground or if you catch it," Greg said.

Scarlett shot the cookie toward the hoop. It hit the rim, broke apart and fell into a bed of impatiens. "We could give it to Percy…" She bent to pick up the pieces.

"No!" Lena said. "Honey, chocolate is very, very bad for dogs. Didn't you know?"

"Oh, it is?" Her face fell and she stood there with the cookie pieces in her hand. Daniel's heart flipped in his chest, at the way her innocent mistake troubled her because she'd never had a dog of her own. "By your expression," she said, "we're not just talking the same way chocolate is bad for children."

"It's poisonous, if they eat enough of it," Lena explained, "and Percy is pretty small. It wouldn't take a lot to make him pretty sick."

"I'm sorry. I'm so sorry!" She dropped the cookie pieces back in the bed of impatiens. "Just imagine if I'd given it to him without talking about it first…"

"You wouldn't," Lena reassured her. "You would have asked."

"I still have a lot to learn about puppies." She threw a

look across at Daniel, her cheeks pink with a remorse that he found completely adorable. He was in serious trouble, and right now that seemed like the best place in the world.

Chapter Ten

"You're looking much better, honey," Scarlett's mother, Helen, said, across the restaurant table on Saturday evening. "This vacation is doing you good. Even Dad noticed, although don't expect him to say anything."

"I wouldn't want him to," Scarlett said. "We'd be bound to slide into difficult territory."

"Very true, you probably would. He's not big on admitting when he's wrong. So I won't say anything more. Just pleased about the color in your face, that's all, and that you're getting some of your curves back."

She glanced to her left at Scarlett's father, seated at the end. He was having one of his typical conversations with MJ, full of one-upmanship and ego. MJ was seated on Mom's right, so that the conversation cut right across her, and it was loud and focused enough that Dad hadn't heard what Mom had said.

"I'm glad it shows," Scarlett said to her mother, while

wondering if it was really possible that the two men enjoyed relating to each other that way. She glanced in their direction just as Mom had.

Look at them! They were both dressed in expensive suits, both seven or eight inches over the average in height, and both inclined to use the advantage it gave them. It was a toss-up which of them was taller. She wouldn't have been surprised to find them standing on tiptoe to ensure a win in that area. Dad's hair was steel-gray and MJ's was dark, but apart from that they seemed so similar.

She caught Andy looking across at her, with a twinkle in his eye, as if he knew what she was thinking. The champagne he'd ordered arrived at their table, and the waiter set out the glasses and prepared to open and pour.

There were seven of them gathered here tonight— every adult in the McKinley family, including Claudia. The four women were dressed up for the occasion, with blonde Alicia and brunette Claudia in designer dresses, Mom in a gray-and-mauve-patterned skirt and blouse, and Scarlett in black pants, heeled sandals and a draped, silky soft top that matched her name.

There were no kids, because Alicia and MJ had brought their full-time, live-in nanny, Maura, up with them from New York for the weekend, and she was at their motel with their two children, Abby and Tyler, and Claudia's baby, Ben, as well.

Claudia, on Scarlett's left, kept checking her cell phone for text messages, because she'd been adamant that if Nanny Maura had any problems with the baby, she *had* to get in touch right away. Andy had already told her twice that Ben would be fine, and she'd conceded that, yes, she was worrying too much.

So no kids, and also no Daniel, because Scarlett didn't want to go public on their relationship when she had no idea where it would lead. She'd said this to him today, and as usual he hadn't said much in reply, just agreed with a brief line. "Whole lot of reasons why it could be awkward." He'd been sitting on the floor of his living room as he spoke, with Percy playing in his lap. "Plus I have this little guy to take care of today."

The puppy had settled in well, so far, although Greg and Lena had warned them that he might be a little needy and sad overnight for the first couple of days, missing his mom and his familiar environment.

Daniel and Scarlett had spent the whole afternoon setting up a bed and a litter box, shopping for puppy food and treats, showing him the great outdoors at his new home, under close supervision. Daniel planned to fence in a run for him, with access to the garage space he was clearing out. That way Percy would have plenty of indoor and outdoor space during the hours when Daniel wasn't at home.

Scarlett had torn herself away very reluctantly when it was time to come home to Andy's to greet her visiting family, and was a little alarmed at how attached she'd become to the puppy, and to the shared activity of caring for him, when a dog was such a new thing in her life.

She was spooked—and she knew Daniel thought she was overreacting—about her mistake with the chocolate, and if he knew she was planning to buy a book on the care and training of puppies, he would probably laugh.

But tonight was about Andy and Claudia, not Scarlett and Daniel, even if she couldn't get him out of her head. Andy had asked the rest of the family to come up from New York because he had "something to announce," and it didn't take a great deal of detective work to know what that something was, especially given the fact that he was wearing a suit like the other two McKinley men.

He'd brought them all to this very nice French restaurant in a neighboring town, close to the motel where MJ and Alicia were staying, and had ordered the champagne which was now flowing into the tall flutes and being passed around. When everyone had some, he stood up and reached across the corner of the table for Claudia's hand. "I don't suppose this is a surprise to any of you, but I hope it's a pleasure. Claudia and I are getting married in October."

Mom burst into tears and hurried around the table to hug her future daughter-in-law, making little cries of joy and excitement. Her candy-floss gray hair made a silvery contrast with Claudia's dark head as they came together. MJ and Dad both stood and left their seats, too, clapping Andy on the shoulders and vying with each other to be the loudest and most enthusiastic in their congratulations.

MJ was really *too* enthusiastic. It sounded false, and Scarlett didn't understand why he would need to be that way. Envy? It almost seemed that way, and yet what did MJ, of all people, have to be envious of? He had the perfect life, with a successful career, a ton of money, a beautiful home, a healthy child of each sex and a stunningly beautiful wife. "What's the plan, bro?" he almost shouted. "Are you moving back to the city?"

"Claudia is moving up here," Andy said. He looked at her, then back to MJ. "She's done all the research on setting up her own business, now, in accountancy and financial planning, and there's a vacant office and a good child-care center right near my practice, which will help us organize the family schedule." He said the word *family* with a casual air that fooled nobody. He was loving his role as an instant dad for Claudia's baby, and he couldn't hide the fact.

"A proper wedding?" Alicia asked, of no one in particular. She ran her fingers up and down the stem of her wineglass, then adjusted the shoulder of her nutmeg-brown silk jacket. "Is there time to organize that by October?"

"It's not going to be a major undertaking," Claudia said to her. They were seated directly across from each other, with Andy at the end of the table in between—or he would be, when MJ and Dad let go of him. "Elegant, but small. Whatever we can manage in the time frame."

"Why have a time frame? Why not take longer?"

"We didn't want to push it back into the cold weather, or wait until spring, so we decided to make the wedding fit with the dates, not the other way around."

"Don't make it too small, though," Alicia said quietly. "Don't cheat yourself, on such an important day."

Scarlett heard, but she didn't think anyone else had. Mom was grilling Andy, now, about when and how he'd proposed. She was very suspicious that maybe he hadn't done it properly, with the right romantic setting and words.

Scarlett couldn't hear Andy's answers, but it didn't look as if he was managing to allay Mom's concerns. She heard the words *motorcycle, clown suit* and *hot-air balloon.* Maybe he was teasing. Claudia certainly didn't act as if she had any complaints. Meanwhile, MJ and Dad were talking about reception venues, and how to negotiate the right deal on the drinks, arguing as usual.

"MJ and I did it on the spur of the moment, in Las Vegas," Alicia went on to Claudia. "And… Well, it just wasn't special enough. It was tacky, some of it. It makes me feel sometimes as if we're not really married, even though the paperwork says we are."

"I'm all about the paperwork." Claudia laughed. "So that's not a problem."

"But I'm so embarrassed about my wedding photos, I never show them to anyone."

"Alicia, you look stunning in your wedding photos,"

Scarlett couldn't help saying. "Completely and utterly stunning."

Because it was true. Alicia was one of the most beautiful women Scarlett had ever seen, with her classic Scandinavian coloring, perfect bone structure and beautifully shaped eyes and mouth. Her figure was gorgeous, too, even after two pregnancies. She worked out with a personal trainer in an exclusive gym almost every day.

But Alicia didn't agree. "I was wearing a cocktail dress, off the rack and not even new. I hadn't had my hair done. MJ's cheeks were all flushed. We'd just been out to dinner. It was an impulse. It was—" She shook her head. "I could have managed it better."

She narrowed her eyes and disappeared inside her own thoughts, and Scarlett was left with the usual feeling that she didn't really know Alicia at all, even though she and MJ had been married for seven years. That was an odd phrasing at the end, there, too. *I could have managed it better.* Not "we" but "I."

MJ had heard it, also, seated back beside his wife, leaning back in his chair. He was frowning, the way he did when someone said something he thought was foolish or wrong. MJ shared their father's name—Michael James McKinley—and so many of Dad's character traits. Neither of them suffered fools gladly.

Did he think his wife was a fool? Scarlett wondered. Had the charm of her beauty worn thin? Surely there was more beneath the beauty for him, though? She realized that not only didn't she know or understand Alicia, she didn't understand the marriage. Was it happy? What made it work, if it *was* working? If it wasn't, what had gone wrong?

Shoot, it wasn't something to undertake lightly, a marriage. She, of all people, knew that, with a divorce under her belt by the time she was twenty-six, and an ex-husband she would happily never set eyes on again.

She shivered at the thought. Kyle hadn't called again, but she kept expecting it. She was certain that first phone call was only step one in a planned strategy. The possibility of step two hung over her like a sword on a string, whenever she thought about it.

Kyle was the kind of man who needed the social convenience of being married, but who didn't have the capacity for real passion, in directing his quest for a wife. He would go for what he saw as the most sensible and straightforward option, she was sure, and if he thought he had a chance at rekindling his first marriage, then he'd sensibly try that first, before moving on to the messy business of finding someone completely new.

Scarlett thought that Andy and Claudia would almost certainly make their marriage work. The evidence wasn't only in the way they looked at each other, or the way they always seemed so aware of the other's position in any room. It was more about how they'd handled all of the practicalities so far. They hadn't rushed into a decision about meshing their lives together, they'd thought everything through, aware of the fact that they had a baby to consider as well as their own needs.

They had a lot in common, and some differences that gave a balance to the relationship, because they respected those differences and met each other halfway. Andy was more easygoing. Claudia believed in attention to detail.

What about Mom and Dad? Scarlett wondered.

They'd been married for thirty-eight years, so they had to be doing something right. But there were tensions, too. Of course there were. Mom thought Dad should cut back his workload, or even retire. She wanted some quality time with him while they were still young and fit enough to enjoy it. He took vacations in grudging three-day chunks, while she wanted to tour Europe or see the Rockies and even China or Australia.

Right now, Dad was getting flushed from the champagne and talking too loud. Mom kept putting her hand on his arm, across the corner of the table, in an attempt to tone him down, but he shook her off without looking at her and eventually she sat back with a sigh and picked up her menu, as if to say, *If it's up to me to enjoy my evening without your help, then I will.*

Scarlett realized that she had seen that exact sequence of behavior from her parents too many times before.

Andy had sat back down, now that Dad and MJ had finished the manly hugging and slapping and shouting. He looked across at Scarlett and asked her quietly, "Have you said anything to Dad yet about the fact that you're not just on vacation? That you've actually resigned?"

"Not yet. He'll want answers, and I don't have them."

"No? I approve of the steps you're taking to find them, though. And I don't just mean working with Aaron Bailey."

"Oh. Right."

Andy told her even more quietly—only Claudia would have heard—"You should have brought him." No prize for knowing who he meant by *him.*

"No…" She couldn't hide from Andy or Claudia that she was seeing Daniel, when she disappeared to his house in the evenings and didn't return until the next day, or when his car was parked in Andy's driveway all night. This past week, they'd only spent Friday night apart, and her brother would have been blind not to notice.

"Why not?"

Scarlett blushed. "You like your dinnertime sport bloody, then."

"Why?" Andy demanded. "What would have happened?"

"With you two all champagne-toasty and blissful, what would Mom have done? Asked Daniel and me all sorts of embarrassing questions so she could work out what we were up to, and if we were heading in the same direction. I hate that you two even know something is happening. I wish nobody knew!"

"Why is it so shady, though, Scarlett?" Claudia asked, her attention drawn to the conversation. "You're both free to have whatever kind of involvement you want. You're consenting adults."

"That's just what Daniel said, even though he agreed it was probably better if he didn't come."

"So what's the problem?"

"I just don't want it under a microscope. I don't want the whole family marrying us off and planning our babies when maybe it's—" She stopped.

"Only a fling," Claudia suggested, trying to be helpful.

"Yes. That."

"Your mom doesn't want flings," Claudia guessed. "She wants you married."

"She wants an antidote to my first marriage, and she looks for that in any man she meets who seems even slightly like a candidate."

"I'm not going to ask if Daniel really is a candidate."

Andy laughed. "Claudia, sweetheart, you just did ask."

"I didn't!"

"Right, so if I say, 'I'm not going to tell you that's the fiftieth time already that you've checked for text messages…'"

Claudia made a reluctant face. "Okay. You're right. That *is* saying it, isn't it?" She looked down at her phone and winced again. "Not the fiftieth. Tenth. Take my phone."

She held it out, bravely renouncing addiction. "Put it in your pocket. It's set to vibrate."

"You do realize that Maura has my cell phone number, too? Not to mention Alicia's and MJ's? She has at least four ways of getting in touch in a heartbeat."

"Ah, yes, logic. How I used to love it once, before I became a mom. What happened to me? And is there further horror yet in store?"

"You're cute." Andy pressed his nose against Claudia's across the table.

"So are you." She pressed back. The rest of the world disappeared from their awareness.

Scarlett breathed a silent sigh of relief that they'd apparently forgotten all about her. She heard Mom say, "I think we need to plan for it, Michael. I want a deadline. You can't fob me off and tell me 'just a couple more years' forever. I don't want to tour Europe on a walking frame."

"I don't have to retire for us to tour Europe. There are short packages where you hit the—"

"Michael. Dear. Europe is not a drive-by shooting."

Dad laughed suddenly. Mom's humor could still take him by surprise. She looked pleased at getting the response and the edge dropped from their argument and the positive side of their partnership showed. "I'll take some steps," he said, slow and a little sheepish. "Okay, Helen? I'll look into it."

Mom sat up straighter. "Give me a deadline. Now. While I have witnesses."

"Three years, all right?"

"Three years." Mom looked around the table. "You all heard him. Apparently it's possible. Three years from now, other heart surgeons *will* manage to save a patient or two. The future of Western medicine will not collapse in a heap when Dr. Michael James McKinley hangs up his stetho-scope, thirty-six months from now."

"You're holding me to *months?*"

"I'm not sure if I can book our flights that far ahead, but yes, I am holding you to months."

Two hours later, the meal wound to a close. Alicia and MJ returned to their children, their nanny and their hotel. Andy and Claudia went to the hotel, also, to collect Ben and all the baby gear that he'd needed for the evening. Mom and Scarlett were left standing on the sidewalk out-side the restaurant while Dad, in typical fashion, paused at the bar to query an item on the check, even though he'd already paid.

"I wish he wouldn't do this," Mom said. "I told him he'd misread the waitress's writing, but still he has to make sure." She looked at Scarlett, apparently taking inventory of any signs of unhappiness or stress. How many would she find? "In case we don't get another chance to talk this weekend, darling, tell me how you really are."

"How I really am is great." Scarlett took a breath. "I've resigned from City Children's."

"Resigned?"

And of course Dad chose that moment to reappear, barreling through the restaurant door, the arithmetic on the check explained to his satisfaction. "What?" he said. "What did you say, Helen?"

Mothers! Their conflicted loyalties could really make trouble, sometimes. "Scarlett's quit City Children's."

"Mom—!"

"Honey, he had to know. I'm not keeping that kind of a secret, when I've finally gotten him to agree to the Europe trip."

"You couldn't have let me tell him?"

"Were you going to? Tonight?"

"It doesn't matter when she was going to tell me, Helen," Dad said. His tone changed, impatience giving way to indignation and anger and disbelief. "Scarlett, you were working with Jonas Tisch. He's one of the best pediatric oncologists in the country. Please tell me you've found someone even better—Mark Alexander or Vikram Patel...who else is there?"

"Dad, I don't have another job to go to, yet, okay? I told you I was taking some time. Please trust me on this."

"You have the best brain in the family—"

"You always say that."

"Because it's true. You outscored your brothers on every IQ test we ever put you through."

"*Put me through* being the operative words."

"Are you saying—?"

"I'm just saying I need some time. That's all." She felt her scalp beginning to tighten. "To work out what I want from life beyond exercising my fantastically muscular brain. To work out if my brain really is the most important thing about me. It's what you value about me, Dad, but maybe there are different things about me that I value more."

"Scarlett—" He'd gone red.

"Michael..." Mom put her hand on his arm, the way she always did.

"Helen!" He shook her off.

It was ridiculous, all of it. There was nothing more to say, and all three of them seemed to recognize the fact at the same time.

"We need to get to the store before they close," Mom reminded Dad. "You need those anti-inflammatories for your shoulder or you won't sleep, in a strange bed."

Scarlett took her keys from her purse. "I'll see you at Andy's."

But she felt restless as she drove off, and had only a moment of indecisiveness at the first turn. She wasn't going to submit to more bullying from Dad tonight, or more of Mom's flawed attempts to mediate. So she took a left instead of a right, and headed for Daniel's place, because right now all she wanted was the certainty of his bed and his warm, strong body.

Chapter Eleven

Daniel heard Scarlett's car in his driveway at just before ten o'clock, and his pulses jumped. She'd said she wasn't coming tonight, after the family dinner, and yet here she was. He met her at the door before she could knock and then he didn't know what to say.

I've been thinking about you all evening.

Come to bed.

Marry me.

Maybe all three.

She looked so beautiful in that slinky, silky red top and those figure-hugging black pants, the heels of her shoes emphasizing the lean length of her legs. And as for the look on her face… She was eager and impatient and embarrassed and doubtful, all at once. She was unsure of her welcome, uneasy about what she might be giving away.

Lord, she should walk a mile in *his* shoes!

"I didn't know if…" She stopped, and he knew it was up to him to give her the right words.

Not *marry me*.

That was crazy.

"Hey… Come in." It was gruff and too short—the same length, in syllables, as *marry me*—but it was all he could come up with.

"Should I?"

"You're here, aren't you?"

"Do you want me here?"

Marry me.

"Of course I want you here. I think Percy missed you, too."

He didn't understand, not really, why she wanted to be here, that was part of the problem. His feelings were completely simple in this situation and he knew that that wasn't going to work. It just couldn't be that simple. He probably would have said it if he'd thought she was at all ready to hear it.

Marry me.

But you just didn't say it at this point. You'd be crazy to.

And he knew she wouldn't want to hear it. Especially after her divorce, fresh in her mind since Kyle's phone call. She would want way more certainty than this. Way more certainty than he could offer her. Way more proof that it made sense on paper. He knew nothing other than what he felt and the strength of that.

"Percy missed me? He did?"

"Well, he's been whining a bit. Missing his brothers and sisters, and his mom. He's asleep in his basket for now. Take a look."

She did, peeking at him from a distance so as not to waken him. "I just love him. How can I have gotten so attached so fast?"

Yeah, tell me about it…

Daniel had no idea where the *L* word fitted in. Whether she would want to hear that. Whether it would be true.

What did it even mean?

As for the *M* word, he had no idea if that was some thoughtless, shallow, knee-jerk reaction, the kind of thing he had seen in the course of his work a couple of times, played out in courtrooms and emergency rooms and county offices. People sometimes said it too fast. *Marry me.*

And then *did* it too fast. And had kids. And got divorced. And said it and did it again, and had a second divorce, so that you ended up with ugly scenes in family court and mixed-up kids and shattered finances and just a whole lot of mess and regret.

How did you know? What did you trust?

"But do you really? Want me here? Your mind is somewhere else. Can we stop looking at the dog, so I know?" She stepped close, and he pulled her into his arms and buried his face in her. In the scent of her. The warmth, the softness, the familiarity and rightness.

"Can't you feel how much I want you here?" he said against her neck.

"That's a relief. For a moment… You weren't saying anything much, you were just looking at Percy, and I thought—"

"Don't be dumb. Sorry I wasn't saying anything."

"Got anything to say now?"

"Not much. Come to bed. Your top is great."

He touched her, all the places he loved and the places he wanted to know better. The row of hard little knobs that was her backbone, where she still seemed too thin despite the weight that was starting to come back on. The creases at the tops of her thighs, which he'd discovered were incredibly sensitive to the feathery exploration of his fingertips. Her ribs, running up to the undersides of her breasts, where he felt the texture of satin and lace. Was this a member of the underwear team that he'd met before, or was it new to him? He couldn't wait to find out.

They stopped trying to talk, which was a relief. Words were such a risk, sometimes. You said the wrong ones and you couldn't take them back. You explained and made it worse.

His body wasn't nearly as clumsy as his language. His body couldn't lie, not to Scarlett, and it could say the most momentous, true, powerful things without her even realizing it. Things that were so true *now* that he couldn't even begin to wonder if this meant they would still be true next week or next month or next year. How did you know? What did you trust?

She arched against him and sighed out a heavy breath. "Oh, Daniel…"

The great thing about a small house was that it was never that far to the bedroom. They reached it in stages marked by kisses in the living room doorway, kisses leaning against the corridor wall.

Her top was so silky against his hands, and the way it was draped made it easy to slide his hands inside it right where he wanted. It slipped from her shoulders and the bra was the same bright lipstick-red and apparently the wrong size. It barely contained her.

"You knew you were coming here all along," he muttered. He kissed the soft, delicious mounds. "Evidence is right in my face…"

"I probably did." She arched again. "Pretended I wasn't. Fooled myself for a while. But then Dad was pressuring me about stupid stuff and I cracked."

She kicked off her shoes, dragged down her black trousers, and there was a little matching red boy-cut lace stretchy thing, with her cheeks peeking half out of it the way her breasts peeked out of the bra. He explored all the places where fabric met skin, until she gasped at him, "Take them off."

So she was naked while he was still clothed, and he was quickly impatient with that, pulling at his shirt and jeans and the rest of it and making them disappear into a heap on the floor with record-breaking speed.

The room was dark, but the size of it and the shapes in it distracted him for a few moments, all the same. None of it seemed good enough…grand or ornate or special enough…to echo the power of their connection.

Scarlett had never commented on the difference between this place and the home she'd grown up in. Daniel kept it neat and clean—there was enough rusty mess in the yard, he didn't want clutter and dirt in the house, too—and he had replaced the battered old furniture with new pieces for his mom's sake when he'd moved back here three years ago. Still, though, there was a contrast. She'd told him she liked the quilts and the photos, but he didn't know how much that meant.

"I changed the sheets," he said to her, as a kind of apology.

But he soon wished he'd kept his mouth shut. She pulled away and looked at him, frowning, holding him in place with her hands on his shoulders. No words, just the frown and the hands and the searching look that said, *what are you* talking *about?*

He tried to cover for the break in mood. "They'll be cool. And smooth."

See? Words made things worse.

Again she didn't answer, she just began to kiss him, and the kisses were a kind of language, they said so many different things.

Relax. It's okay. This is good. Don't ever apologize. Don't break this. Let me just touch you, and tell you with my body, and make you burn.

Kisses soft and slow and juicy on his forehead, his eyelids, his mouth, his neck, below his ear, on his cheekbones, his nose, back to his mouth. Staying there. Staying endlessly, while she pressed into him and rocked her hips and found the right soft place for his erection to rest between their bodies while her nipples pebbled against his chest.

He grabbed her bottom and shaped it with his hands, loving the lush femaleness of it. He kissed her from the soft place low on her belly, up to her breasts and her neck. He ached to be inside her, moving with the rhythm that matched her breathing and sent her over the edge. He wasn't going to last much longer and neither was she. They weren't very good at going slow at this time of night. Slow came later, in the early hours, when they woke up in each other's arms and their kisses were half asleep.

He fell back onto the bed and pulled her on top of him and she opened her legs and braced herself and her breasts moved back and forth and he tried to catch those hard little buds in his mouth once again, until the heat and wet that surrounded him pulled his attention away. Pulled it up and up, hard and fast, until he was gripping her and she was clawing him and crying out and saying his name and they both lost it, just let it go, let it fly and fly.

Perfect.

Always.

How could it possibly stay that way?

Sunday morning…

How Scarlett loved Sunday morning, now that she didn't have hard, unanswerable questions about her patients driving her out of bed, no matter which day of the week.

She shut off the thought, unwilling to go there. She hadn't made any decisions about the future yet. Something told her that she wasn't ready for decisions, and that she mustn't pressure herself, let alone submit to any pressure from Dad. If she did, her fragile recovery from burnout would shatter. Any time her thoughts trespassed in the direction of hospitals, medicine, decisions, she felt the triple prospect of migraine and appetite loss and sleeplessness lurking in the background, and the only way to get rid of it was…

Well, was lying right beside her, with his arm flung across her body and his hair softly prickling her shoulder, his breath warm against her breast, his legs heavy and tangled with hers.

Sunday morning in bed with Daniel.

Yum.

Just yum.

She stretched a little, then relaxed back against the sheets and pillows, and closer into his body. He was sound asleep, his steady breathing *whooshing* in and out, his body so lazy and warm. She had no desire to wake him up or move or get out of bed. She could just stay here for hours, more at peace with herself than she'd been in she couldn't remember how long.

Not thinking. Not wondering or worrying. Just feeling. Just being.

With Daniel here, she felt as if nothing bad could ever happen, because even the worst things would be livable if she had him on her side. With Daniel here, she didn't need to or want to think about anything beyond now…

Until she remembered her parents, staying over in Andy's spare room, while she was supposed to be living next door, there.

Her heart sank.

And it didn't make sense because Mom and Dad weren't easily shockable or repressive about things like that. She remembered how MJ and Alicia had shared a room in a Florida vacation rental with the whole family one Christmas, very early in their relationship.

That's right, Scarlett hadn't thought about this incident in a while. Mom had said privately to her about Alicia, "How long is she going to last, I wonder? I think she's only interested in his money and status. He'll see through that." They'd all been a little shocked when MJ and Alicia had come home from Las Vegas married a month or two later, but Mom hadn't been shocked about them sharing a bed.

So why? Why had this wonderful sense of peace and safety and rightness fled away, now she had remembered that she was supposed to be at home?

Daniel must have felt the tension in her body. He stirred and opened his eyes, saw her watching him and gave a slow, sleepy grin. "Still here?"

"Are you surprised? I was here every time you came back from checking on Percy." The puppy had been by turns active and playful and fretful and hungry, during the night. Daniel had had to get up four times, but he'd insisted that Scarlett should stay in bed.

"Not surprised," Daniel said. "Pleased. Very pleased..."

"I shouldn't be still here, though. Andy is making brunch for everyone this morning."

"And you have to be punctual for that? I gotta tell you, punctuality is against the brunch code."

"My parents will know I stayed. Stayed here, with you."

"And that matters? Your dad's going to come after me with a hunting gun?"

"No gun." But yeah, it was Dad who was the problem. "He'll think—" she tried to work it out, speaking the thoughts as they formed "—that something like this shouldn't be part of my therapy."

There was a silence, while they both considered this. Scarlett realized that Dad wouldn't think she should be using the word *therapy* at all. No child of his—intelligent, capable, in control—should need therapy, for heaven's sake!

Daniel meanwhile had gone on a different track.

"But it *is* your therapy," he said. "I'm therapy." He didn't like the idea. He didn't need to say it out loud for her to know.

Again, she had to think, and finally told him, "I can't explain why that's not bad, the way it sounds. You are the best therapy. Incredible therapy. Like Percy will probably be therapy for you, on a bad day." They thought about that. "It's still wrong, isn't it?"

"Yep."

"How do I dig myself out of the hole?"

"Don't know. Your problem."

She shifted, sitting up a little to look at him. "Don't. I don't want it to be a problem at all. Not yours or mine. In no sense whatsoever did I intend to put you in a box of therapy ingredients, along with the Vermont summer, and working with Aaron. You're…way more than that. You're *good* for me."

"So is therapy good for people. Doesn't mean I want to be that for you."

"In that case, by that definition, every friendship, and relationship, and parent-child bond, and piece of sibling support is therapy."

He thought for a bit, then let out a breath. "Yeah, okay."

She had to laugh. "What? That's it?"

"Well, you're right, when you put it like that. And when I think about Percy."

"So we're not arguing?" she asked.

"Not anymore."

"Good. I think."

"You like arguing?"

"I like finding out if we agree," she corrected him.

"So are you late for this brunch?"

"Slide the clock around, I can't see it." It was sitting on the bedside table, angled wrong.

He slid it, looked at the numbers and told her, "Ten after nine."

"I am late for this brunch. Andy said before nine-thirty. Claudia said she'd be up early with Ben, and she's making muffins and bacon and eggs." She almost asked him, *will you come, too?* But something made her hold the words back.

He rolled out of the bed and grabbed a towel that was hanging on a hook behind the door. "I'm taking a shower. Unless you want to go first."

"We could shower together…" She held her breath.

He grinned. "Much better idea."

She was quite late to the brunch, as a result.

Chapter Twelve

Andy met Scarlett at his front door. "Listen, I don't know if I needed to do this, but I told Mom and Dad you were sleeping at Judy Bailey's last night. I said Aaron was away and she gets nervous on her own and she'd called to ask you to come over."

"Wow. That's…elaborate."

"I know. And probably stupid. I don't know what hit me, it just happened."

"This morning?"

"Last night, after they got back from those errands at the store on their way home from the restaurant. They asked where you were, and why your car wasn't in the driveway, because you should have gotten here before they did." He shrugged.

"Sorry I'm a little late, by the way. Daniel has a new puppy, and—"

And the puppy has nothing to do with why I'm late, but he makes a convenient excuse.

"It's fine, we're running late, too. We've only had orange juice and fruit. Tell me, though, did I need to lie for you?"

"I—I don't know. Probably helps. You would have been caught out if I'd arrived with him in my car, just now."

"Was that a possibility?"

"I almost asked him to come, but then I thought—" She pressed her lips together.

"Dad has really done a number on you, hasn't he?"

"It's not Dad. Not just Dad." She added, "Would he dislike Daniel that much?"

"You know the answer to that. He would think Daniel was too much a part of this whole blowing-your-career-by-taking-time-off stunt that he thinks you're pulling."

"And that I'm not pulling?"

"That you needed to pull. I think you need Daniel, too."

"As therapy. We were having an argument about that exact thing about forty-five minutes ago."

"Come out the back. We're sitting in the sun. We don't need to dissect your relationship with Daniel right this minute."

"You mean it can wait till this afternoon, when Mom and Dad leave? Oh, good!"

"If you want, I'll make sure the man's name never passes my lips again on pain of death."

"What a brother. Always willing to go the extra mile. As far as *death*."

"Come out. You should taste Claudia's raspberry muffins. She learned them from her stepmother and they're great." He led the way, energetic and zesty and content in his casual Sunday shorts and polo shirt.

She envied him, although he'd had his share of troubles in the past, with a dependency on prescription medication several years ago, that would have blown his life and his career out of the water if he hadn't made some major changes just in time.

Dad undervalued Andy, she thought.

Because he wasn't MJ, basically.

And Dad valued MJ because the two of them were so alike.

That's not how it has to be, Dad, she wanted to tell him. *You can value the ways people are different from you, not just the ways they're the same.*

But Dad didn't see it. Within a few minutes of her arrival in the backyard, where an outdoor table and chairs sat in the dappled shade from a huge old oak, he was saying to the gathering, "Doesn't feel safe on her own at night? Couldn't they get a dog? She shouldn't depend on asking favors like that. Scarlett, you should have said no."

Andy mouthed, "Sorry," at her, and she managed to change the subject before Andy's white lie was exposed.

Claudia brought out her raspberry muffins, and Alicia held Ben while she and Andy went back for the dishes of scrambled eggs and bacon, the coffee and the toast. "Aren't you getting pretty?" Alicia said to the baby, but her eyes traveled more often to her own children, Abby and Tyler, who were kicking a ball around with their nanny, Maura, in a corner of the yard.

"That's great, Tyler!" the nanny said, in her strong Irish accent. "You're gettin' it now, precious."

Tyler at two wasn't very good at it, and his four-year-old big sister quickly grew impatient with him. It began to develop into a fight, and Alicia looked as if she was sorry she had the baby in her arms, because it meant she couldn't jump up quick enough to intervene.

She looked toward MJ, as if she might hand Ben over to him, but he shook his head and wouldn't hold out his arms for the baby. "Maura's handling it, Alicia. Just sit.

You can't relax if you're supervising her all the time, and I can't relax, either, watching you itching to step in." There was a mix of tenderness, authority and impatience in his voice.

Alicia gave a little nod and sat back, the very model of an obedient wife listening to her husband, and Scarlett found herself wondering the same thing she'd wondered last night. What was Alicia really *about,* underneath? Had she just married MJ for his money and status, as Mom had suspected years ago?

Maybe no one would ever know.

Unless there was a divorce.

She gave a little shiver. That wouldn't be fun for anyone, especially not with the kids involved. At least she and Kyle hadn't had children to worry about.

Dad was still grumbling at her. "Weakness. That's what it's about, Scarlett. You and this Judy woman with her fears about being alone. You can't give in to it. This is the problem, nowadays. Everyone just makes excuses. I'm telling you, you have about two more weeks for me to pull strings at City Children's and get them to tear up your resignation, but that's it."

"Dad, I don't want you to pull any strings." She spoke as calmly as she could. "I'm happy with my decision."

He glared at her. "What's next, then? What the hell is next for you, Scarlett, if you're just going to waste everything you've worked for?"

And that was when she lost it. "I am not going to waste everything I've worked for! I'm more than just a brain, Dad! I'm a whole, complicated, feeling, irrational, illogical, living, breathing *person.* My whole life, you've been proud of my IQ scores, and my college grades, and my work ethic, and the letters after my name. And that's great. But can you please be proud of something else about me?

That I know how to laugh and love? That I want to explore life, not just run on the same track? That I cut my losses when something isn't working? That I *think* about family and feelings and don't just take them for granted? That I make mistakes, and learn from them? Can you? *Please?*"

Oh, hell, oh, damn, oh, shoot.

She'd hurt him. Or just shocked him so much he had nothing to hit back with. She was his little girl, his only daughter, and his pride in her wasn't a bad thing, it was just too narrow, that was the problem, and, yes, she had hurt him. The rest of the family looked on in uncomfortable silence at the whole thing, while their eggs began to get cold.

Dad blinked, looked instinctively at Mom for support, blinked again. "That's…unfair, isn't it?"

"Yes," Scarlett said. "But you've been unfair to me, too. I love you, Dad. I love that you've been so proud of me. But it's been a *problem,* too, and I'm trying to get past that, and I want your support, not your condemnation."

"You've always had my support."

"I know. But it's been conditional."

"You want it unconditional."

"Yes."

"So what are you planning, if you're not going back to City Children's?"

"I don't know yet, and I want your support with the fact that I'm taking some time to make the decision."

He turned to Mom again. "Helen—?"

"Dear, if you're asking me if you have to take this from our daughter, then I'm afraid I think she's right. You do."

"You have my support," Dad said slowly, looking older and less strong than she wanted him to. "I don't understand you, but I guess that's the age-old way between parents and kids. We raised you, and we should trust you, and we do."

"Thank you." She looked around at her family—Andy and Claudia in their glow of love, Alicia and MJ stiff and uncomfortable, trying to hide it by focusing on their children. "Please eat, the rest of you. I think we can resume normal transmission at this point."

Was it good that she'd said all that? Would Dad ever truly understand? She didn't know, but she thought it was progress.

"This is hard," Paula said. She rocked back on her heels and looked at the box of clothing accessories she'd opened up.

"I know," Daniel answered. "I thought it would be easier with two of us." They were both in the garage on a Friday morning, after his sister had arrived last night. She was staying until Tuesday afternoon, with the goal of making as much progress sorting through their mother's things as they could.

She looked at him, after what he'd said. "It is easier. I wouldn't have let you do this on your own." Her eyes were red-rimmed, her jeans dusty and her hair—as dark as his own—decorated with a cobweb. They'd both cried today, sorting out the remnants of their mother's life. There were so many reminders of good things and bad, so many small and large decisions to be made.

He wanted to give her some words of appreciation, but as usual they were hard to find. "I'm glad you came. You're good. Hope that husband of yours knows it."

"He does." She smiled, then sighed. "I wish Jordan could have come, too, but I think he's working eighty-hour weeks." She reached up to her hair, found the cobweb and fought at it. "Oh, yuck…"

"I had an email from him. He says there are some toys he wants us to hang on to."

Paula surveyed the stacks of boxes piled in the garage. "They'll be in there somewhere."

"Coffee break?"

"Coffee, but let's work through. I just want—" her voice fogged "—to do all my crying by the end of Sunday."

Daniel's throat went scratchy. "Yeah, I think we can get through it by then. What's here in the garage, anyhow. Not sure about the rest. It'll be a long few days. And the yard is a whole different story."

Paula stood up. "The cars… Can we just call some-one and have them hauled away for scrap? Isn't that what you've always said?"

"It is what I've said," he told her slowly. "We can do that. I half want to. The rest of me… I have a friend who likes them."

Scarlett. She was supposed to be getting here any minute. He'd told her that he didn't need her help. Didn't *want* it, actually, and she'd understood about the need for privacy, just him and Paula.

Oh, and Percy. Greg and Lena had loaned Daniel one of their plastic wading pools to give the puppy somewhere to play where he wouldn't get in the way or get himself into trouble, but even though it had slightly higher sides than the one the puppy had been in with his brothers and sisters, he was growing as fast as he knew how, and he'd probably be able to climb out of it in another few days.

He was attempting this feat right now, yelping and scrambling up the plastic sides, in a corner of the garage. Scarlett would have been laughing at him, distracted by him, if Daniel had let her come.

She'd understood why he didn't quite want her, but she'd told him, "You'll need help taking things away, though.

I can do that. It's not so personal. It might help. I'll come by for a load a couple of times a day, take it wherever you want."

He still hadn't found a way to show her that he appreciated the thoughtfulness of that.

"Would he buy them, then?" Paula was asking, about the cars. They left the garage and went up the steps onto the front deck, heading for the house and the kitchen. Daniel had put Percy in his litter box, with successful results, and now it looked as if he was settling in for a nap.

"She," Daniel said in answer to his sister. "The friend is a she." Most definitely a she. "*Appreciates* them, I should have said. She made me see… I mean, they were the only things that Dad ever—" Shoot, why couldn't he do this? "That ever seemed to take him out of himself in a healthy way."

"Oh. Gee," his sister drawled. "You're saying the drinking wasn't healthy?"

"See, that's what I mean. The cars could have been the antidote to the drinking, except that he never quite made it that far. He fell short."

"He fell short in many ways, Daniel."

"Maybe if we—" *Shoot!* "—you know, *respected* the cars, instead of hating them. If we tried to separate out the ones that are worth something. Sell them for a decent amount, and give the money to charity."

"A charity that aims to combat alcoholism?"

"Yes. Exactly."

His sister said slowly, "That's a really good idea. That is such a good idea." She wiped away tears, again, with quick impatience as if they only got in the way. "That would make something right and good, out of the whole mess."

He saw Scarlett's blue car appear beyond the trees that

lined the road and turn into the driveway. "This is the friend," he said.

"The friend?"

"The friend who started me thinking we should do something good with the cars."

"The she-friend."

"If you want to put it like that."

"I'm eager to meet this she-friend."

"Well, you're going to." He knew Paula was looking at him curiously. Too bad. She'd just have to work things out for herself.

Scarlett shut her engine, climbed out of the car and came toward them. "Why do I always get here when you're standing on your front deck, Daniel?"

"Perfect timing, I guess," he said. "This is my sister, Paula. Paula, this is Scarlett."

"The friend," Paula said, with a raise of her brows.

"The friend," he agreed.

"It's nice to meet you, Scarlett."

"Thanks, and to meet you, too. What friend?" Scarlett came up to him and they squeezed each other's arms and he wanted to kiss her but not if she didn't want that, in front of Paula. He couldn't tell, and there wasn't a way to find out for sure, so he stepped back.

"We've been talking about the cars," he told her. "We're going to sell any that have value and donate the money to charity. I told her you were the one who started me thinking on that track."

"Hey, you're giving me too much credit. I never thought of donating the money to charity."

"I would have *paid* to have someone take them away, until that day when we walked all through them and found the DeSoto and the Dodge."

"I remember that day," she said, and he saw the start of

a smile that quickly went away, because it was too private for Paula to see.

It was two weeks ago, now, that day. Two weeks and a puppy ago, to put it better. He couldn't believe Scarlett was already three weeks into her month in Vermont. Only a little more than a week until she was planning to return to the city.

Had her plans changed at all? They weren't talking about it. He had no idea if she'd decided anything yet.

And he was—yeah, okay—spit-scared to ask.

"I've found a few more classic models since then, in good enough shape to restore," he said. "And there are still some rows and piles I haven't looked at."

"You're focusing on the house and garage, you said, while Paula's here."

"That's right. We're just breaking for coffee, are you staying?"

"You wanted me to come for a load or two, that was all."

"You can stay for coffee. You and Paula have barely said hello."

Paula pricked up her ears at this. He knew her. She was wondering, now, just the way Lena had, last weekend. Was Scarlett someone she needed to get to know? Someone she needed to like, or even love?

"Stay," Paula said. "We were going to work through, but we were up and started by six-thirty, maybe we do need a break."

So they had coffee, and some conversation, which consisted of the women talking and Daniel sitting back thinking that it seemed to be going okay as far as he could judge. Then they loaded up a full car's worth of boxes for the charity store.

"I'll come back at five or so?" Scarlett said. "For another load?"

"That would be so good," Paula told her, and gave her a hug. "So?" she asked Daniel, the moment Scarlett had left.

"So we should get back in the garage."

"You are not getting away with that."

He bit the bullet and asked, "Did you like her?"

"I am prepared to love her with every fiber of my being, if you want me to."

"Okay, so you liked her," he tried.

"I asked you first."

"No, you did not. You said the word *so*."

"You could translate."

He said to the sky and the trees, "I forgot what sisters were like."

"Okay, I won't nag."

"Good."

There was a silence. Paula pulled another box in front of her and tore off the tape that held it shut. "You do realize, don't you," she said, "that you are supposed to reward me for not nagging, now, by telling me what I want to know."

"Would if I could. Don't have any answers."

"I don't know how she can stand you."

"I don't know how she can, either."

Chapter Thirteen

For Paula's last night at Daniel's on Monday before she returned home to Boston and her husband, Rob, they went out to a restaurant to dinner, the three of them—Paula, Daniel and Scarlett. It was a simple, family-style place, offering grills and pasta and hearty portions of dessert, because by this stage, Daniel and Paula were way too tired for anything fancy.

Scarlett liked Paula a lot. She was a smaller and slightly fairer version of her brother, in looks, with the same strong shape to her face and the same smile. Although Daniel was the eldest, Paula bossed him around when she needed to, and he bossed her back.

They were blunter and more interfering with each other than Scarlett was used to, and much closer to each other than she was to MJ. Closer, even, than she was to Andy, although she considered that her sibling relationship with him was healthy and good.

She guessed that the closeness, the honesty and the interfering all came from the burdens and challenges the two of them had had to shoulder growing up. An absent and inadequate father, a much-loved mother who was first ill then widowed then even sicker, not much money, and a clever younger brother whom they wanted to protect and help.

It had been good for her and Paula to get to know each other in the course of taking carloads of boxes to the charity store or the recycling center. They had practical things to say to each other, along the lines of, "Is that too heavy for you to carry on your own?" Easier, in many ways, than a purely social interaction.

Tonight was the first time they'd actually sat down together since that first coffee break on Friday, and by now they were much more relaxed with each other, with more to think and talk about than just those two guarded assessments: Does Paula approve? How serious is this woman about my brother?

"We've done so much," Paula said. She'd finished her chicken-fried steak and was looking at the dessert menu. "Are you feeling it's do-able now, on your own, Dan? Do you need me to come back at some point, if I can?"

"No, I'm good. I know it's hard for you to get the time. If I can get some time off work, and hire the 'dozer so I can move those wrecks for the scrap metal dealer, separate out the restorable cars from the junk… The DeSoto is sold already, I couldn't believe how fast that one went."

"I know! It was great."

"Or how much it fetched. I've had some calls about some of the others. I've opened a new bank account for the money, Scarlett, I don't think I told you that. Don't want to lose track of the amount, since we're giving it away to a good cause."

"It would be pretty easy to forget how much it added up to, if it was coming in bit by bit," Scarlett agreed.

"I would come again, Danny," Paula said suddenly. "But I'm starting fertility treatment. I should tell you. So you understand why. That my priorities are split."

"Oh, it's got to that point?" Daniel responded. "Ah, sis…I knew you'd been trying for a while. You've had tests?"

"It's okay. Don't overreact. Yes, we've had tests. Doctor thinks we need some help, but we have a good chance. I'm not even thirty, yet." She turned her mouth upside down. "I'm told the injections aren't fun and I'll be as moody as hell. Lucky you met me now, Scarlett, not a month from now."

"It's been great to meet you, moody or not," Scarlett said honestly.

"Don't even think about coming back, in that case," Daniel told his sister.

"No, well, certain times of the month Rob and I are obligated to be in the same space or the injections won't achieve much, so it would be tricky."

"Yeah, too much information, thanks."

"You can handle it. Rob and I have been married for five years. But don't worry, I'm changing the subject now, so you can relax. Scarlett, when do you head back to New York?"

"Next week. Is when I planned to." She spoke awkwardly, less comfortable with this new subject than the previous one. "My apartment is empty. I'm very flexible. I can head back whenever I want. Or extend. For a while."

"Might you do that?" Paula looked at her across the table, and her dark eyes were a little too interested in the answer.

"I'm not sure. At some point I do have to decide something. About my career. Further study."

About Daniel.

About what he wants.

About what I want, and what's possible and sensible and good.

"You're a children's cancer specialist and you want *more* study?" Paula was saying.

"I could switch specialties. I've been thinking about the possibility. Something with less pressure and better hours. Or I could move to a smaller hospital."

"In Manhattan?"

"Anywhere."

"You have no idea about any of that?"

"I'm still thinking."

"Don't think too much," Paula said. It seemed cryptic. Or else too perceptive.

The waiter arrived to take their dessert orders, and her perky inquiry came as a relief. Scarlett ordered something involving death by chocolate as an antidote to the tension she could feel inside herself when Paula tried to gain an insight into her plans. She appreciated that it was friendly interest—and maybe a little sisterly protectiveness, too— but she just wasn't ready, and the unreadiness had begun to scare her more with each day that went by.

Maybe Dad had been right, after all, to question the extent of this break from her regular life. Maybe it was creating confusion more than decision-making and certainty. Maybe she was throwing away the best thing she had.

How did you answer these questions? She hadn't had a migraine since that first one had almost blasted her off the road three and a half weeks ago. She could feel the sense of health and well-being returning to her body. She'd put on some of the weight. She loved working in Aaron's studio. She was *happy*.

Surely happiness should come with certainty and an ability to see the way ahead.

So far, it didn't.

So far, she was left with the sight of Daniel's sister hiding her doubts in a massive slice of peach pie à la mode, and Daniel himself looking at her as if she was a hand of poker and he mustn't give anything away.

The only place either of them seemed to give anything away was in bed.

Scarlett went home to her own, that night, and missed Daniel's body beside her the way she would have missed water on a hot day or a warm coat in winter. She ached without him. She felt incomplete and full of doubt and just miserable.

Tuesday night, after Paula had left, she was back in Daniel's bed at his place, with Percy snuffling and wriggling and snoring in his basket on the floor.

They slept in the same room, the three of them, until the end of the week, mostly at Daniel's. But then on Saturday morning in Scarlett's bed at Andy's house, less than a week before she was supposed to go back to New York, there was suddenly—heavy and warm on her feet and waking her up—a puppy who had discovered he could climb onto the lower shelf of the bedside table, and from there to the bed itself.

Daniel woke up and came to the same realization. He swore. "This was not in the plan."

"Yeah, about that. I thought the plan was the garage at your place and the laundry room at mine."

"Well, he really is going to start going in the garage, but he's still so little. How can we banish him from the bedroom, when he's only just stopped crying at night?"

"He can't be that little if he can climb onto the bed."

"How angry are you?"

"I'm only angry at myself. For thinking he's so cute that I don't even care about the black hairs on the quilt, even though it's my brother's."

"Good, because I don't want to have to move to get him off the bed, right now."

"Did I say anything about you moving? Well, I mean, you can move, but…"

"I can move?" Daniel nestled her closer into his arms and they both looked at the puppy at the foot of the bed. He'd curled up in an inky ball and was going to sleep, highly satisfied at his accomplishment, and at what it had delivered in terms of immediate benefits.

"Like that, you can definitely move." They settled into an entwined shape every bit as comfortable as the puppy's. "What are you going to do with him, when he's bigger?" Scarlett asked lazily. She felt a jolt deep inside her as she wondered if she would be here to see the dog as he grew. She had to make some kind of a decision soon.

About whether to sublet her apartment.

About how long she could afford to stay between jobs.

About what she hoped she and Daniel might decide.

Decisions *soon…*

Very soon.

But not now.

"Well, keep him, of course," Daniel said, just as lazy.

"That's not what you meant."

"I meant, is he going in the backseat of your car, with his head stuck out the window and his tongue catching the breeze?"

"Some of that, for sure. I'll take him fishing. The fish will be happy about that. He'll splash so much, they won't come near close enough to get caught. We'll go jogging.

He'll help in the yard, when I've had the ground smoothed out and I'm planting some trees. I really like the idea of turning the whole four acres back into woods, the way it once would have been."

"But you're selling it."

"I like the idea of it, even if I'm not there to see it. It'll be easier to sell if it has something more than bare ground around the house."

"You think he'll be good at planting? I love the idea of trees. Sugar maple, and yellow birch and spruce."

"Dogwood and cedar, too. Hoping he'll help with the holes."

"He may have his own ideas about the holes."

"You somehow seem to think that I'm a total pushover for this dog."

"Gee, where's my evidence?"

"Okay. Point taken." He rolled out of the bed before she could grab him back, picked up Percy, put him in his basket and moved the basket, and the food and water bowls, to the corridor outside the bedroom door.

Which he then firmly closed.

Before coming back to bed, as naked as he was when he left. "This is where I'm a pushover," he said, bringing his warm hands in a long slide all the way up her body. "This is where I have no willpower at all."

Scarlett gave him no argument on that one.

When Scarlett and Daniel finally surfaced, his stomach told him they'd well and truly missed breakfast. Percy was scrabbling at the door, and he realized that the little guy's litter box was down in the old-fashioned scullery that opened off the kitchen.

"You're a good man to wait," he told the dog, because

there were no telltale puddles or odors anywhere that he could find.

Dressed only in his boxers, he took Percy downstairs and put him in the box, then saw the glint of sunlight on a car windshield and discovered a sleek red vehicle turning in from the street.

He raced back up the stairs. Scarlett was in the shower. He knocked on the door and called to her, "You have a visitor."

"Not Andy?" she called back.

"You mean not *for* Andy? No, the car's in the driveway on this side."

"Huh," she said. Daniel heard her turn off the faucets and push the shower curtain aside to reach for her towel.

He went into her bedroom and pulled on yesterday's jeans and gray polo shirt. The jeans-and-polo combination—different pairs, a range of colors—was getting more wear than his uniform, right now, as he'd managed to switch rosters and have the past two days off for shifting the cars with the bulldozer he'd hired. Downstairs, the doorbell sounded just as he'd pushed his feet into a sockless pair of trainers, and he went to answer it, convinced it would be someone with a pamphlet or a collection can.

It wasn't.

It was a smooth-looking male of around his own age with an air of entitlement that matched his city-casual clothing, and an enormous bunch of flowers in his hand. He asked for Scarlett, and Daniel distrusted him on sight. Was this—?

Yeah, it was. Of course it was.

Kyle. Her ex.

Scarlett didn't even have to say his name. She came down the stairs with a towel still in her hand, drying the hair she'd had time to wet but not to wash. Daniel saw the tension enter her face and knot into her shoulders, saw the way her body froze and her eyes shifted.

"Oh, please, no…" she hissed under her breath, then out loud to the visitor, "You didn't call, Kyle. Or send a text."

"I emailed." He handed the flowers to her with a flourish, and added, "For you."

"I haven't checked my email since yesterday." She was too flustered and unhappy to thank him for the flowers. They poked up out of their swathe of paper and looked too bright and too crowded together, like gate-crashers at a party.

"No, I can see you've been…busy." Kyle was smiling, but the look he gave, from Daniel to Scarlett and back again, didn't contain amusement.

"Yes, I have been busy," Scarlett said. "Kyle, this is Daniel Porter, a—" she made a tiny, telltale pause "—friend." She was trying so hard to gather herself, but it wasn't quite working. She reached back and put the flowers on the hall table. "I'm not sure why you're here. And you have no right to be angry simply because I hadn't caught up on the fact that you were coming."

"I'm not angry." Oh, but he was. Daniel could see it glimmering darkly behind the urbane facade.

Well hidden.

Actively denied.

But there.

It set his teeth on edge. He could recognize that the man was good-looking. Athletic. Well-groomed. Well-heeled. He had a heck of a lot to offer, in anyone's estimation, and he was far too confident about it. He reminded Daniel of too many things that were lacking in his own life.

Money, for example.

A stellar career track.

A high-level college degree.

Of course the guy had a sense of entitlement. He might be a jerk, but he was entitled all the same.

"This is downtime for me," Scarlett said. She sounded overcareful and defensive. "I'm not checking my email that often. And as I said, you had other ways to get in touch. You didn't even hint when you called a couple of weeks ago that you might be coming up this way."

"And as *I* said, Scarlett, I'm not angry…"

"I am," Daniel cut in. Because how could he not be angry, when the guy was everything he himself was not?

Kyle cast him an irritated glance disguised as a courteous smile. "Scarlett and I have a few things to talk about. I'll introduce myself, Daniel." He stuck out his hand and when Daniel shook it, Kyle deliberately gripped painfully hard. "I'm her ex-husband. Could you give us some time, please?" The polite manner was like fingernails on a chalkboard, like someone cutting glass.

Like the way Kyle would talk to waiters or garage mechanics or hotel porters.

"Kyle, I'm sorry," Scarlett said. "I don't need time with you, private or otherwise. You shouldn't have come."

"I thought you might be interested to hear that Julie and I have split up. I don't think we got to that on the phone, the other day." He spoke in the same falsely casual, half smiling way in which he might have informed her he'd won twenty million in the lottery, like he expected it to change everything. It was throwing him totally that Scarlett wasn't alone, Daniel could tell.

He couldn't imagine that a man like Kyle would be thrown by his—Daniel's—presence in many other circumstances.

"We didn't get to it," Scarlett said. "But I'd heard. I'm sorry to—"

"Don't be sorry to hear it. You know the marriage was

flawed. I did it to get back at you, but that was wrong, and I've learned a lot from that."

"Have you? That's great, but I don't know what it has to do with me."

"Of course you know. You're too smart not to. I think we have a real possibility of constructing something positive, now, and I'd like to start that process. Carefully, of course. Our marriage always had far more going for it than we were able to access at the time. But we can't talk with—" He glanced sideways, and Daniel could almost hear the unspoken end to the sentence.

With this goon hanging around.

Pink spots of color had appeared on Scarlett's cheeks, and her voice was strained. "There's no process, Kyle, careful or otherwise. There is no possibility of us getting back together. Ever. I need to make that clear right now."

"You can't know that until we've talked."

"I can know it. I know it to my bones."

"You're not thinking it through. You're not giving it a chance."

"Any thinking through has been well and truly done on this side of the equation, six years ago."

"If you're using the word *equation,* then you're confirming that there's still—"

"There's not. Please. Don't argue this as if it's just a question of getting the semantics right."

Semantics?

Shoot, Daniel thought, two people could use that word when they were talking about anger and separation and possibilities? What the hell was he doing listening to it?

"I want you to listen to me." Her voice shook. She was getting more rattled as Kyle persisted.

Percy made his presence known. He had an opinion, apparently. He skittered out from the kitchen and up to

Scarlett, who was standing between the stairs and the front door on the polished hardwood floor.

The floor was slippery and Percy didn't like it. He climbed onto Scarlett's feet and started scrabbling at her bare legs the way he'd scrabbled earlier at the bedroom door. She was wearing shorts, and the puppy's claws were getting thicker and stronger as he grew. He left white, papery scratch marks on her skin.

"Oh, Percy, no, not now," she said.

But Daniel approved of the puppy's intervention. "Take him," he said to her. "I think you should."

He didn't trust himself, if she stayed. He didn't trust her, either. She was going to keep talking, and complicate things with words, instead of simply slamming the door in the guy's face. He could see that she was sincere about it, that she was trying so hard, that she was being clear enough that any reasonable man would listen, but it didn't help, she shouldn't be doing it.

The whole way Kyle looked at her and spoke to her and made slick, self-satisfied and grotesquely wrongheaded assumptions about their marriage, divorce and possible reunion tied Daniel in knots of anger. He wanted a few words with the man alone. He wanted to make the kind of argument that Kyle couldn't possibly ignore.

And yet he distrusted himself. Would Scarlett want him to muscle in like this, like a paid protector?

He controlled his voice, focused on the puppy for a moment in order to gather himself. "He needs the back-yard and some food. He's making a mess of your legs, Scarlett. And you need some space. Kyle and I can say anything that needs to be said. There's not much. He'll be out of here, soon."

"I have an opinion about that," Kyle said.

"I'm sure you do," Daniel growled at him.

Scarlett nodded, chewing on her lip, and picked up the dog. "You're right, Daniel. I need a moment. I need—" she seemed like a completely different person in her ex-husband's presence "—air."

Folded in on herself.

Frozen.

Second-guessing every word she spoke and every movement she made.

Daniel thought that the only reason she'd agreed to the plan to take Percy outside—why she'd taken the cowardly approach, basically, by leaving Kyle to him—was that five years of marriage and an unpleasant divorce had stripped her of her last vestige of capability in a situation like this. She was making a doomed attempt to stay tolerant and cool, and the effort was breaking her.

Daniel didn't consider, at the moment, that tolerance and cool were required.

Chapter Fourteen

Scarlett could hear the two men—their raised voices, cutting each other off.

She could even hear some of the words.

Percy was snuffling around the shrubbery and the lawn, discovering a thousand unique and fabulous smells. Scalp tight and tingling with tension, she followed him and kept watch over him, the way MJ and Alicia's nanny, Maura, had followed little Tyler when he first learned to walk, because he wasn't safe on his own for a single second.

Percy snuffled around to the side gate, while Daniel and Kyle were standing on the front porch, just out of sight beyond the corner of the house. Scarlett could hear them more clearly from here. She listened helplessly, as she tried to regroup.

Daniel called Kyle a clueless idiot and a stalker. Kyle called Daniel a redneck. And worse. Way worse.

Should she have stayed?

But seeing Kyle just dragged her back into the old patterns with a relentlessness that scared her, making her feel as if she hadn't grown or changed at all. She hated that so much. She realized how Kyle had always rewarded her for the exact same thing that Dad did—her bright mind—and that she'd fallen for it at first because it was familiar, it confirmed all her tried-and-true reasons for self-esteem.

But she *had* changed since their divorce. She'd challenged Dad about his attitude, and she'd begun to explore new ways of living, new ways of thinking about herself, new qualities to value in herself and others. In Daniel, especially.

"You're acting as if you have something to offer her, Porter, but you don't," she heard Kyle say. "Your worlds and your backgrounds and your aspirations are poles apart. Think about it."

"I have. Trust me."

"Sure you have. Of course you have." Kyle's voice rose louder. "But you're not thinking with your brain, buddy, you're thinking with your—" The last word, Scarlett didn't catch, but she could guess. "And so is she, the—" *Shoot!* He'd called her *that?*

She heard the squeak and thump of feet on the wooden planking of the porch, heard a *thud,* and the sound of a man's breath leaving his body too fast. Angry feet sounded on the bitumen of the driveway. A car door opened. Which meant that Kyle was at least conscious and upright.

She had to see what was going on.

She bent and picked up the puppy and told him shakily, "Let's go, shall we? Let's do this."

She fumbled with the catch on the gate and got it open. Kyle was shoving himself into his vehicle, now, revving the engine in his angry haste to get it started. She could see him beyond the sun glinting on the car windshield, his pale, smooth face carved out of rock as he struggled to regain the calm and intellect that contained his whole self-identity.

He saw her and watched her approach, and she knew she couldn't let him think for a single second that her reappearance was any kind of capitulation. There had to be no wiggle room. She shot out her words as if they were bullets. "Kyle, this is over. I am not interested. I can't make it any clearer than that."

"Fine," he said tightly. "You're behaving like a child and you're completely irrational about it, while I'm trying to use my actual brain, but you've made your point. And so has your piece of beefcake, there. Rest assured, I won't be back."

He gunned the car in reverse down the driveway, and Daniel appeared near the sidewalk out front, watching him go.

He was clutching his right fist in his left hand.

On woolly legs, Scarlett went to him, with Percy in her arms. "What did you do to him?" she asked shakily.

"I didn't punch him." He watched the retreating vehicle with an odd look on his face, a mixture of anger and satisfaction and something else that she couldn't read.

"Hang on, you *didn't* punch him?" she said.

"I wanted to." He turned away from his view of the street to look at her, his eyes clouded, his forehead in a tight frown. "Shoot, I wanted to, so bad! Had him pinned against the wall. He was going to fight back, I'll give him that."

"He goes to the gym. Prides himself." She couldn't talk about it—Kyle's cool, smug attitude to his own physical fitness.

"Yeah, I could tell he thought that was going to be enough," Daniel growled.

"But it wasn't going to?"

Daniel sketched in graphic terms that it wouldn't have been enough, and why. He went to the gym, too. He ran and swam. And he thwarted violence for a living. "But then I took control of myself. Didn't want to break my hand." Again, he squeezed his fist with the other hand. "Hell, I still want to hit him. Maybe I should have." He was half talking to himself.

"You had him against the wall." They walked back to the house. Scarlett still had Percy in her arms. It was so weird and funny, the puppy as a counterpoint to what had happened. He was writhing like a snake and wagging his tail. He just loved his humans, and everything they did. They were going in the house! Maybe there'd be food and toys! "I heard a sound from him as if you had hit him, as if you'd winded him."

"I swung back," Daniel said. "But then I got control of myself and pulled it. He reacted. Grunted. It was instinctive, I guess. Then he ducked and ran. I let him. Just wanted him out of my sight. No man is going to call you that. No man is going to tell you he wants you back, and then call you those things." His fist tightened again, pulled up in front of his chest so that it made his bicep bulge. "Shoot, I'm starting to really wish I had."

She laughed, still a little shaky, and said what she felt, without even thinking. "I've never met anyone like you, before." Because it was true.

"No?" he growled in answer. "I'm not so different, am I?"

"Anyone so—" Where were the words? Her feelings

were so strong, beyond her ability to capture or describe. "Raw," she tried. "Simple. Basic."

The words fell into the air between them a little clumsily.

"Yeah, well," he muttered. "Sometimes it just is simple."

"Yes…"

He looked at her, his gaze clouded. "Can't apologize for that, Scarlett. Can't apologize for a whole lot of things." He stared outward, away from her, at something in the room that she couldn't see. Something that wasn't physically there. His body still gave off the aura of frustration left by the punch he'd managed not to throw. His eyes were narrowed and his mouth hard and closed, lips pressed together. His big shoulders were held tense and tight.

She felt shut out, when she wanted to fling her arms around him and feel their connection. "Want to eat?" she suggested.

It brought his focus back. "It's late," he said, looking at her with those eyes still narrowed and distant. "I have that 'dozer waiting at home."

"Right. You probably need help with all that."

"One-man job, pretty much. It's taking a while, even though we've sold several more of the cars. I need to get it done. Paula and I talked to Jordan. He feels the same as we do. We've started, we have a plan, let's deal with it."

"Let me come out later, then. I can bring dinner."

"No need." Why wasn't he *talking*?

"I want to," she insisted, in case he honestly didn't know.

"If you really do." He looked at her from a distant emotional place that she didn't understand, and she couldn't find a way to bring him closer. Where was the simplicity they'd just talked about? The honesty that they'd given each other, up until now? The intense, zinging power of their shared attraction?

She was feeling quite shockingly, blazingly honest after the sickening glimpse into the traps of the past that Kyle had given her. If Daniel had given her the slightest inch, she would have jumped into bed with him, or told him—

Told him she loved him.

Lord, was it true?

Did it make any sense?

She felt it, in an overwhelming rush that needed to be spoken out loud, and yet she didn't say it—couldn't— because Daniel had put some kind of an emotional force field in place. His whole body was pushing her away, loud and clear. She didn't buy the talk about the machine waiting for him. Not at all.

She loved him, and he wanted to play bulldozers. He'd just saved her, like in a fairy tale, from Kyle-the-emotional-dragon, but he didn't want the fairy tale reward, and none of it meshed.

"I really do want to help," she said. "But you don't seem to want me to. I'm not sure what's going on."

"Don't push, Scarlett."

She swore. It didn't help.

He gave her a skeptical look. "Let me call you about dinner, okay? I might not be fit company."

"Okay."

And with that, he went. Took his puppy and just went, leaving her without the slightest idea of what had gone wrong.

Maybe it was stupid to let that jerk get to him, but Daniel couldn't help himself. He drove home with the dark cloud of it hanging over him. A jerk the man might be, but that didn't mean he couldn't hit on the truth occasionally.

Especially when it was a truth that Daniel himself had known all along.

You're acting as if you have something to offer her, Porter, but you don't.

And then Scarlett had pretty much said it, too—that he was different, and she'd never known anyone like him. He was...what were the words she'd used?

Raw. Simple. Basic.

Yeah, that stacked up well against rich, successful and clever, didn't it?

It sealed the deal. Sealed his understanding of the truth.

She deserved more. Not every guy with Kyle's background and assets was a jerk.

At home, he gulped a bowl of cereal and a banana, made sure Percy was settled after the exciting trip in the car, put on his safety helmet, too impatient to fasten the strap, and went out to the bulldozer. The landscape of cars had changed a lot since he'd started on it Thursday, but there was still a long way to go. The earth looked raw and tracked up from his comings and goings, and the piles of wreckage for scrap were growing in size and number.

Surveying the scene, it struck him for the first damned time in his life that this was actually a beautiful piece of land. Or it could be, one day, in the right hands. The semirural outlook, the undulating green of the terrain, the distant views of mountains. If he planted some trees, even a buyer without much imagination would be able to see the potential. Someone was going to be lucky with this place, when those cars were gone.

He couldn't afford to keep it, himself, and his brother and sister had no use for it, with their lives elsewhere. To hold on to it, he would have to buy Paula and Jordan out, and he didn't think the bank would look kindly on the idea, as things stood. His mother's illness had cost a lot. He barely had anything saved.

You're acting as if you have something to offer her, Porter, but you don't.

The words kept drumming in his head. Kyle had said other things, worse things, but those he could discount, those came from a desire to hurt and a position of defeat. He could discount the analytical reasoning, too. Kyle had enumerated the problems using his fingers like bullet-points in a formal presentation.

Scarlett had higher-level education, Daniel had a two-year community college degree. Scarlett had a stable childhood and a ton of parental support at her back, Daniel had poverty and alcoholism and family illness. Scarlett had status and prospects and choices, Daniel had honor at best.

But he couldn't doubt the simplicity of Kyle's conclusion, or his own.

She deserved more.

Every time they were together, the same two momentous words crowded into his mouth.

Marry me.

Now, he wanted to laugh at himself about it—that he could want to say it with so little to go on. It seemed stupidly naive. Just dumb. Raw and simple, just as Scarlett had said. Raw and simple was fine for a short while, but it didn't get you very far in the longer term.

He saw his aching sense of love like an illness no one had recognized or diagnosed. "Poor guy, he didn't know he had it, and it killed him, just like that."

This wasn't going to kill him.

But it was killing something, as he worked on, out in the sun.

Killing his sense of healing about the cars, his sense

that life had entered a new chapter, and that Mom would have been happy.

He wanted to ask for the moon with Scarlett, but he felt that he had no right and no backup.

Nothing to offer, just as Kyle had said.

He pushed and dragged with the 'dozer, finding a kind of release in the noise and vibration, the dust in the air, the crunch of metal against metal, the gradual opening up and orderliness of the terrain. He must have been at it for hours, by this point. It was probably time to take a break and grab something to eat and drink, but he kept going because of the release, because it helped with the pain and frustration of the whole stupid *marry me* thing that he couldn't get out of his head.

Daniel, what were you thinking? Push, grind, drag. *Who were you kidding?* Crush, turn, heave. *What did you hint to Paula, that had her looking happy for you? That there was a future in it?* Veer, crunch, pull. *And now you'll have to tell her you were wrong.*

The 'dozer protested. He was asking too much of it, the way he was asking too much of himself.

Tough. They could both keep going for a little longer. He didn't want to stop until he was numb with weariness and unable to think, and that hadn't happened yet. He was still thinking way too much.

Grind, bulldozer, grind. He pushed it forward once more. It tilted on the dirt and one wheel ran too high up the pile of metal. At almost the same moment he saw a flash of metallic blue color in the front yard beyond the house and recognized Scarlett's car.

Oh, shoot, how was he going to handle this? He'd made it pretty clear he didn't want her here today. What was he going to say? His distracted thoughts jolted and veered off in a new direction, and he did the wrong thing with the gears, gunned the machine forward instead of back. It made the machine rear up. The whole thing was totally his fault.

Even while it was happening his focus was still half on Scarlett, although he'd lost sight of her. She must be coming toward him, and had disappeared behind the house or a pile of cars. But this stupid machine...

No, it wasn't the machine, it was him. The result was the same.

It tipped on the pile of metal.

And began to fall.

The engine died with a whine, the unfastened helmet flipped off his head, and Daniel thought he heard a woman's scream—Scarlett's scream—right before the pain hit his leg, his head hit the ground and he blacked out.

Scarlett froze. The bulldozer lay on its side beside Daniel, who didn't move. She had the sense not to run to him blindly—he must still be fifty yards away, or more—but to scrabble through her purse and find her phone to call 911. Then she desperately tried to talk sense to the operator with the phone pressed to her ear while she began to race forward with stumbling steps.

"I don't know if he's conscious." Her mind wouldn't let her imagine anything worse than unconsciousness. It was a blessing that she could see him now that the piles of scrap weren't in the way. "I just saw it happen. I can't believe I saw it. If I hadn't come..."

But even as she said this she knew it was wrong. It had happened *because* she'd come. Because she'd spent the past five hours thinking about the way they'd parted from each other this morning, the way he'd pushed her away with no explanation, and she'd finally known that

she had to take action. She had to push back, find out what
he thought and tell him he was wrong.

And now look what had happened. He'd seen her and
had reacted so strongly to her presence that he'd been distracted and lost control.

She managed to give the address, and the operator told
her to stay on the line. Scarlett begged her, "I'm a doctor,
but this is someone—this is a friend. Help me to keep my
head. Talk me through this for a little longer. Please."

She reached him. He still hadn't moved. She dropped
to the bare, tracked-up ground beside him and saw blood,
and then the faint movement of his breathing. She muttered a prayer of bone-deep thankfulness.

Alive.

Breathing.

But unconscious.

He'd hit his head on a blunt, twisted lump of metal, and
it had knocked him out, but that was merciful, because
otherwise his leg…

Oh, his leg. It must have been hit by the falling machine. His body was lying clear of the wheel now, but
the crooked shape of the leg told her it was broken. "He's
bleeding from a head wound," she reported to the 911 operator. "His leg looks to be broken in two places, above
and below the knee. He's breathing but unconscious." She
dredged up the E.R. training she so rarely needed now, and
tested his response to light, which was better than she'd
dared to hope.

"The ambulance should reach you in around fifteen
minutes," the operator said.

"That long?"

"I can stay on the line with you the whole time, if you
want."

"No… No, I'm okay. I need to see what more I can do

for him. I need both hands." She disconnected the call
and focused on Daniel's beloved body. If she could have
splinted his leg here on the ground with her bare hands
she would have done it. If she could have taken his place,
she felt she would have done that, too.

She had to do *something*. She was a doctor. She—

Didn't feel like a doctor. Felt like a woman distraught
because the living body that was so precious to her was
flung on the ground like a rag doll. His jeans were covered in dirt. His T-shirt was ripped and twisted. His eyes
were closed, and she had to fight not to kiss those eyelids
and tell him uselessly, "It's okay, I'm here."

You're a doctor, *Scarlett.*

"Daniel, I'm going to look at your head. I'm going to
sponge away the blood. The ambulance is coming. I'm
here and I'm not leaving you."

In her purse, she found the cosmetic-size water spritzer
that was part of a birthday beauty gift basket from Alicia
and sprayed it onto the wound, then dabbed it with a wad
of tissue. There wasn't much bleeding, and the injury
didn't seem to go deep. What more could she do with it?
Not much.

Words seemed so useless. Emotion had nowhere to go.
"The ambulance is going to be here any minute, Daniel.
Hang in there. Stay with me." Action, where was the
action?

Maybe words weren't completely useless. "Stay with
me, Daniel. Come back to me."

He groaned deeply then opened his eyes. She sobbed
with relief. His vision was dark and cloudy and confused
and pain-filled, just the way hers had been that first day a
few weeks ago. He didn't speak and then the full awareness of the pain rushed into him and he groaned again
and the eyes rolled back in his head while the lids quickly

closed, but the moment they had been open was good, it made these last minutes bearable.

She sat cross-legged on the ground beside him, with one thigh pressed against the warm side of his body. She talked to him and took his hand. The strength in it was absent, just gone. It nestled limp in her palm, and she had to take the weight of his forearm across her leg. "Stay with me, Daniel, you're going to be okay. Just rest. You're on the ground. You had a fall. I'm here. I'll always be here. I'll be here forever if you want me, here on this land, anywhere you want me. Oh, Daniel. Oh, hear that? The ambulance is coming."

His face was peaceful and still, the unconsciousness making him mercifully oblivious to the pain for now. She traced every line and texture of that face with her eyes, helpless about it. Those lids, those lashes, the corners of his mouth, the straight length of his nose, the dust and beard stubble and sweat sheen on his cheekbones. He couldn't push her away when he was in another place, like this, and she felt so close to him, almost a part of him.

How could a man's body be this precious to her?

How could she belong to it, and to him, so completely?

She felt that she would do anything, cut off her own arm, hold him like this until the world ended. It went beyond any logic or words. It went beyond sex or anger or misunderstanding. It was so certain. It had mixed itself into the chemistry of her bones.

If he didn't feel it, too, then she understood nothing about the world.

What had Kyle called him? Her piece of beefcake? That was so wrong, in so many ways. Yes, Daniel's body was utterly precious to her, but that wasn't a shallow thing. It was *everything*. She'd seen how empty a mental connection could be, when the passion and the emotion weren't there. She didn't want that again, the way she didn't want Dad's insistence that her brain should dictate the work she did.

Daniel's body was the vessel that contained his spirit, and she wanted to cherish that vessel with everything she had, for as long as she could.

As long as life lasted.

If he would let her.

Was *that* why—?

He wasn't planning to let her.

Shoot, yes! She remembered something else Kyle had said, something about Daniel having nothing to offer.

Daniel believed that, she realized, and not just because Kyle had said it. He'd always believed it, deep down. He'd believed it six years ago and he believed it now, and Kyle's words had confronted him with the familiar idea in a way he couldn't ignore.

She heard the sirens growing stronger, and saw the ambulance at last. Everything was confusing after that. The paramedics took over. "He's going to be fine," they told her. "He's starting to come round and we've given him something for the pain. We'll temporarily splint the leg."

"Thank you. Thank you so much." She didn't say again that she was a doctor, because it seemed so unimportant against everything else.

They wrapped her in a blanket as if she was the one needing treatment, and made her sit in the back of the ambulance, and in the quiet she had to confront how she felt.

She'd left him alone all day. She'd agonized over the way he'd left this morning, but she wanted to give him some space, because surely that had to help. She'd cracked at around four, driven over so that he couldn't fob her off over the phone or leave her hanging by not answering a text.

And then she'd seen him working on that bulldozer as if he had demons to drive off, and maybe he did. Was she going to let him drive her off at the same time? The sick, desperate feeling in her gut gave her the answer.

She believed in what they had.

She believed in how right it felt when they were together, not just right for now, but right forever. She just had to find out if Daniel believed it, too. "I'm not the same person I was six years ago, Danny," she whispered aloud. "I'm not going to let this go."

Chapter Fifteen

She was here. Scarlett was here.

Daniel felt her presence with his eyes closed, and saw fleeting images of her when his eyes came open. It was hard to keep them open—everything was woozy and wobbly and indistinct with the effect of his head injury—so he didn't do it for long. And then, when his eyes were closed again, he saw her in his dreams.

She spoke to him. "Aaron and Judy are taking care of Percy whenever I come in here to see you, and he's fine… The surgeons have set your leg. I called MJ and read the orthopedic surgeon's notes out to him and he says it all sounds good. You'll heal like it never happened… Percy is going to need obedience training. He keeps running off with my heart in his mouth, I just love him so much. When I picked him up from the Baileys last night, he greeted me with these little barks… Are you awake, Daniel? No, not really. That's okay… I'm here. I'm back… It's a good hospital, I like it. They think you'll be ready to go home the day after tomorrow. Now just rest."

His leg hurt, and so did his head. He kind of remembered how it had happened. Bulldozer. His fault. Tired and hungry and distracted. Scarlett, so precious, but from a different world. Her ex had said it, he'd known it in his heart all along, and he'd brooded on it for hours. While working on those damned cars. He was supposed to press a button when he was hurting, but he resisted because he wanted to be awake and alert so he could grab Scarlett and—

That was a different kind of hurt.

A harder kind.

He wanted to be alert enough to tell her, "You don't need to do this. Greg and Lena will take Percy until I'm back home. They'll take care of *me*. I'll barely even need to ask, and they'll be there. I'm not your problem. It's not your responsibility, or your role."

She was *his* problem, though.

He wanted everything she was doing, everything she said to him. He wanted to be fully present in every moment when he saw her figure or her face. But it wasn't right. He couldn't remember why it wasn't right, most of the time, but he knew it anyhow.

He knew it holding her hand. He knew it smiling when he heard her voice. He knew it as the need for heavy medication began to wear off, and she was still here, and he was running out of excuses for not saying what he'd struggled to say when he was half under.

This can't work. Not the way I want.

"Go home," he tried. He'd been here for two nights, the nurse said. It felt like longer than that. Or else it felt like five minutes. He couldn't tell. The nurse had said he would be going home tomorrow.

Meanwhile, Scarlett was sitting in the chair beside the bed with his hand in hers, and he squeezed it as he spoke, and then ran the ball of his thumb over the back of it.

"I'm not going home," she said.

"Why can't you listen?"

"Why can't you?"

"To what?" he croaked.

"To what I'm saying without words."

"Don't mess with me." Because he couldn't take it, right now.

"Is that what you think is happening here?" she said softly.

"I have no idea what's happening."

"You're getting better. I'm taking you home tomorrow. And I'm not going anywhere. That's what's happening."

"I can't argue."

"Good."

"Would if I could."

"Then I'm glad you can't."

The next day, he felt a lot better. Scarlett was still there, managing his discharge like the professional she was. He didn't know whether to be terrified by it or laugh out loud.

She was even dressed and groomed like a professional, with her hair pinned on top of her head and a mouth slick with a soft pinky-brown lipstick, and wearing killer heels, a silky pale gray blouse with pearlescent buttons down the front, and a hip-hugging matching skirt. He knew that his body was going to make a full recovery when he couldn't get the questions out of his head about what she might be wearing underneath.

"I have the crutches," she told the discharge nurse, all clipped and crisp and practical. "We'll try them at home. If he's not handling them right, we'll come to Outpatients and work with a therapist."

"At first, though, he won't even want to try the crutches, he'll need—" the nurse began.

"Yes, you're right, of course. The wheelchair. Thanks for reminding me, Alana." She gave the nurse a smile. "Until he's ready for the crutches, I've rented a wheelchair, and I'm familiar with how he'll need to use it. Some of my patients, in the past, have lost limbs due to their illness and have been in wheelchairs or on crutches, so I'm experienced with some of the problems he's likely to encounter."

"Great," said the nurse. "That makes my job easier."

"No problem. Is there anything more he needs to sign, or take?"

"No, you're pretty much done."

"I'll grab the wheelchair from the car."

Wow, Daniel *remembered* her like this! He'd barely thought of it, but this was how he used to see her six years ago. She was only an intern, back then, so the aura of total competence had been a little wobblier, a little more prone to the occasional slippage.

But the package and the mannerisms were the same. She absentmindedly held her purse in the crook of her arm the way she used to clutch a clipboard of medical notes, and she looked at him every now and then with that same fleeting, smoky, not remotely professional glance she'd given him at the hospital in New York City—the one that had made him start saying hello to her, angling for a way to ask her out.

He sat in the chair in his hospital room and waited for her to arrive with the wheelchair and thought how easy it would be just to let this keep going without ever finding a name for it. They'd talked about that, a few weeks ago. They'd agreed a name wasn't necessary.

But he didn't believe this anymore.

At some point, you had to define it, and if you couldn't define it…if you didn't both feel that defining it *mattered*… and changed things…changed everything…then it—whatever it was—didn't last.

There was only one definition he wanted.

The full package.

The *M* word and the *L* word, with the *C* word—children—in the future, but honestly? Kyle was right. A broken leg and a head injury later, Daniel still believed that on this one thing, Scarlett's ex was right, and that Kyle wouldn't be the only one to think that way. Her parents would feel the same. Her work colleagues. Her friends. Her brothers, too.

You tried to put what he and Scarlett had into that complete, classic package, and it just didn't fit. For a whole lot of reasons.

He heard the rubbery sound of the wheelchair on the polished vinyl floor. She was back. "Sorry," she said, sounding breathless. "This thing was a little trickier to get out of the trunk and unfold than I was expecting."

"You sound as if you ran with it."

"Hurried, not ran. I hated to think of you sitting here."

Yeah, well, his thoughts hadn't been the happiest, during those minutes.

It must have shown in his face. She tipped her head to one side and looked at him with her hands on her hips and an impatient huff of air escaping between her teeth, as if she understood exactly what was on his mind. "How difficult are you going to be about all this, Daniel?"

"All what?"

"The next few weeks."

"Aren't you going back to New York in the next few *days?*"

"No. No, I'm not. I'm going to apply for a job in Vermont. Spring Ridge Memorial Hospital is only an hour from Radford. It has an opening for a pediatrician. If that doesn't work out, I can wait. Something else will come up."

"What if I want you to go back?"

"Then you have to say it, the way I said it to Kyle."

"Go back to New York."

"Yeah...no." She tutted and shook her head. "I'm sorry. There's no conviction there." She positioned the wheelchair and stepped closer, to help him up.

He struggled to stand, felt a small jolt of pain and a bigger jolt of stubbornness. "Go back to New York."

She came and took his arm, standing so close he could feel the press of her hip and the warmth of her breath. "Better than that, Daniel," she told him softly.

"Go back to New York." But it was weaker this time, not stronger, the way it needed to be.

Her face was only a few inches from his. She reached up and touched his cheek with her fingertips, then ran them back to his hairline and threaded them upward. His scalp tingled, and the sensation spread outward, all down his spine. Into his limbs. Into his groin.

She positioned her mouth a half inch in front of his lips and dared him with her eyes to resist kissing her.

He couldn't.

His mouth met hers. Met the fabulous familiarity of her softness, her sweetness, her taste, her teasing. She pulled away and left him throbbing for more. He almost cried out at the loss, just managed to hold the sound in his throat so that he ached there, and had to swallow around a hard lump. He sat hard into the wheelchair and jarred his leg, but that kind of pain didn't count.

"Let's go," she said. She had a smile on her face and a stubbornness about her that he didn't trust…and couldn't tear his eyes from.

"He really is a gorgeous little guy," Judy Bailey said, when Scarlett went to pick up the puppy for the last time. They stood in the kitchen, while Percy slept in his basket in the laundry room, just through the open door. "I've loved having him here. Is this it for you, too? You're due to head back to New York…"

"I'm staying," Scarlett said. "If Aaron still wants me, I'd like to keep working here."

"Aaron would love to have you, and so would I. I've been hoping very much that this isn't goodbye. But is it open-ended, your stay?"

"I—I'm not sure. There are…decisions I can't make, yet."

Judy looked at her closely, putting down the coffee mug she'd just drained, and Scarlett felt the color creeping up her neck. "Decisions that depend on someone else, not just you, is that what you're saying?"

"Yes."

"Decisions that depend on Daniel Porter."

"How did you—?"

"You think I haven't recognized your car parked at his place when I drive by?"

"I keep forgetting this is rural Vermont, not New York City."

"He's a good man, Scarlett. When we had a robbery here a couple of years ago and Aaron lost thousands of dollars worth of tools, he was so helpful. I knew his mom a little. You would have liked her."

"I believe you, Judy. I know he's a good man. Problem is, he doesn't think he's good enough."

"Because of his family's struggle? His father was—let's just call it *flawed*."

"He can't see that I only care about him even more because of all of that."

"And you don't know how to convince him?"

"The current strategy is to stick to him like a burr and hope he'll eventually accept that he can't brush me off."

Judy laughed. "You could try the opposite approach. Make him come after you. Men like that."

"Knock his socks off, first." Aaron came through the screen door, bringing the usual aroma of fresh-cut wood. He must have heard the last part of their conversation. "Men like that, too."

"Aaron!" Judy said.

"He's gotta know, in full, glorious Technicolor, exactly what he'd be missing." He grinned, and Judy hit him with a teaspoon. Scarlett didn't know whether to hug him or look for a more effective weapon.

But maybe there was something in his idea...

Helplessly, for the first six hours after he got home, Daniel submitted to everything Scarlett did for him. She set him up on the couch with a heap of pillows. She found three different-size boxes and tubs for him to rest his leg on at different heights, so that his body didn't stiffen up or go numb from too long in any one position.

She brought him a mug of potato soup and a BLT sandwich and orange juice and ice cream. She went to fetch Percy from the Baileys, then brought the puppy to the couch for Daniel to play with, and whenever she wasn't actually in the room, he could hear her tidying up the kitchen, training Percy with his bathroom activities, calling Paula and Jordan and Greg and Lena with updates on how he and his leg and head were doing.

"Now for dinner tonight..." she said at around five. "What would you like?"

"Salmon, with dill and lemon sauce," he answered deliberately, "and homemade potato salad and maybe a nice Caesar salad, too, on the side. I know what you're doing, Scarlett."

"What am I doing? The menu is no problem, by the way."

"I'm not serious about the menu, okay? You're paying me back for when I took care of you, but there's no need, you know that."

"Yes, I do know that. The payback is only a tiny bit of what I'm doing."

"A tiny bit. So, what else?"

She shrugged. "It's what you do, in a situation like this. It's part of it."

"Part of what?"

"I have to go buy that salmon. And maybe we should finish with a chocolate cream pie? It won't be homemade, I'm sorry. Standards have slipped."

"I wasn't serious about the food," he repeated.

"Too bad. I was." She cast him an honest glance that took in the fiberglass cast on his leg, the bandage on his head and what he knew must be a very washed-out look on his face. "And you're not in a position to argue. In fact, if you want to *shift* position, you should probably move to lying down and take a nap."

He very much wanted to argue, but unfortunately she was right. He was wiped. Completely wiped. And he couldn't do a thing about it. He'd been told it was likely that he'd feel this way for another day or two. She left the room and he closed his eyes for a moment and didn't even hear her car starting up, but it must have started, and left, and come back again, because the next thing he knew was that mouthwatering aromas were coming from the kitchen.

She really had cooked salmon, with everything he'd asked for on the side.

"Now you're just showing off," he growled at her. They sat side by side on the couch with the plates on their laps, starting with the Caesar salad and moving on to the salmon in its tangy sauce and the potatoes tossed with mustard and mayonnaise.

His wheelchair was parked beside the couch, and the crutches leaned against one wheel, even closer. The wheelchair was pretty useless in this small place. He wanted to get onto the crutches as quickly as he could, or he'd go stir crazy, he knew.

"And why would I need to do that, I wonder?" Scarlett was saying.

She was driving him crazy with this sense that she'd discovered something, or learned something, or decided something, and she was waiting for him to catch up. "What is it that you think is happening here, Scarlett?" he almost yelled in frustration.

"I think we're getting lost in the same territory we were mired in six years ago, only this time I'm not letting you win."

"You think I won, before?"

She took a breath, stood up, took their empty plates, came back with a huge triangle of chocolate cream pie, on a single plate, with a single spoon. "Actually you're right. Neither of us won, before. We both lost. And maybe it couldn't have been any different back then, but this time it is different."

"It's not. What's changed?"

"What did Kyle say to you?" she asked. She wasn't eating the pie. And she wasn't giving it to him.

"You said it, too. We come from different places, Scarlett. We're different people. So different."

"Does that matter? Isn't it about the place we've met in now, and which direction we want to go in the future? Do people have to be clones of each other, to get along? I know what Kyle said to me. He called you my piece of beefcake."

"Wow." He shook his head. "That's—" A whole other angle, just as damning as everything else.

"And I thought about that. And I saw it completely differently. And it's so clear to me."

"Wish it was clear to me," he growled at her.

"It's going to be," she whispered. "Just you see…"

She picked up the plate of pie, and filled the spoon with a generous mouthful, then slid it into his mouth. Her curled fingers brushed lightly against his chin. Her brandy-brown eyes watched the movement of his lips. She was sitting very close. As he swallowed the chocolate and cream and sweet, crumbly pastry, she slid even closer. "Ready for some more?"

"I can feed myself."

"Tell me you want to, and you can."

But he couldn't say it. She was right there with the spoon and the pie, the sexiest sight he'd ever seen. "My turn now," she said, and spooned a froth of cream and chocolate between her lips, pressing them against the curved metal of the spoon to smear every last taste into her mouth. He couldn't look away. He couldn't speak.

"Mmm," she said, and licked her lips, then scooped up his next mouthful and fed it to him with the same slow, deliberate care.

She took a second mouthful for herself, as the cream and chocolate slid down his throat. He felt the press of her thigh against his good leg. She was perched on the edge of the couch, with her hip angled so that the curve of her butt stuck out like a peach. She fed him another mouthful.

"I know what you're doing…" he said again, through the cream and crumbs. He meant something different, this time.

"So tell me to stop." She took her lower lip lightly between her teeth and looked at him for a moment, then put the plate of pie on the coffee table as if he'd told her he was done. She waited, and he saw the stubbornness in her jutted chin, and the ache of wanting in her body, and a tiny flicker of self-doubt and fear in her eyes.

It was the fear that did him in.

They were so good together in bed, and she was trying desperately to prove something about that, and he knew what it was, and he didn't believe her, but the thought that she was laying herself on the line like this, and that she was *scared* about it…

Every protective instinct in him kicked into life, along with every instinct of another kind. He was powerless against two such strong forces.

"Don't stop. Don't for heck's sake stop until you've damn well finished what you started," he muttered, and pulled her against him so he could reach her sweet-tasting mouth.

Chapter Sixteen

It couldn't help but be a little clumsy, Scarlett was certain.

And the idea of clumsy had never seemed so magical. Daniel's hands, Daniel's mouth, she didn't care how clumsy they were.

They kissed until they were gasping, and then he sat back and slowly unfastened the buttons of the blouse that she still wore from this morning. He let his fingers trail across her breasts, tracing the place where black lace met pale skin, damming back the heat in both of them with the deliberate slowness of every touch.

"Take it off," he finally said.

She was reaching around for the fastening before he even got the words out. She shook the straps from her shoulders and let the bra drop to the floor, then closed her eyes and took a shuddery breath as he reached out and cupped her breasts, then ran his hands down to her waist, and the tight fabric of her skirt. "This, too."

"Have to stand up."

"And you'll have to help me, in a minute." He pulled his T-shirt over his head, but the jeans, with one leg cut off at the thigh to allow for his cast, would be much harder.

"Love to," she told him. "Always."

Always, Daniel, I mean that.

She swallowed the little jolt of fear inside her. She was laying herself on the line so much with this. In so many ways, it had *Last Gasp* written all over it. He was going to try to push her away as soon as it was over, she was certain of it, and she wanted to get in first, do what Judy had said and make him come after her, but she had no idea how she would do that, or if it would work, or if it would end in tears.

Hers.

His, too.

She knew he would hurt himself if he pushed her out of his life, but maybe he was prepared for that, maybe he thought it was the only thing possible. How did you convince a man that you meant forever, when he didn't believe forever could work?

She wriggled out of the skirt, slid her underwear down her legs and found him watching her, his eyes narrowed and smoky and glinting and his mouth poised on a breath. He was going to try to stop this, she could tell. He'd gotten ahold of himself, of his willpower in a last-ditch stand, and he was going to pull himself back and take mental control.

Not letting it happen, Dan.

Naked, she straddled him before he could say the words banking up in his throat. The cast on his leg reached to his thigh and she could feel the hard edge of it against her bottom, while the denim of the jeans scraped her inner thighs and her peaked nipples brushed the afternoon roughness of his jaw. He groaned and let himself go, and for the moment she'd won again.

"This is what happened last time," he said thickly. "Six years ago. It was amazing, and then we said goodbye."

"No, this time it's different."

"Yeah, my leg wasn't set in concrete, before."

"If that's the only difference you see…" She bent and kissed him, then slid upward and gave him her breasts again. He buried his face in the valley between them and she felt the deep, ragged rhythm of his breathing.

"Difference is that you keep fighting me, you keep wanting something," he muttered against her skin.

"I want what you want, only you won't let yourself have it."

"How do you *know* that?" He swore. "Are you just *reading* me? Is it written on my body?"

"I just do know it. When you injured yourself. When the 'dozer tipped over. You were all tied up in knots, and that's why the accident happened. I get it. But can't I tell you I love you and that will be enough? Why can't it be enough?"

"Do you?"

"Yes. I love you."

"What does that mean?"

"It's the name, remember? We couldn't find a name for this, but I've found one. It's love. It's forever."

"Prove it."

"I proved it to myself a few days ago when I sat beside you on that tracked-up ground, with your leg pointing three different directions. Do you know the traditional church marriage vows? Have you ever noticed how *physical* those are? With my body I thee worship. To have and to hold. To cherish. In sickness and in health. Those vows are about bodies. They're about cherishing the vessel that holds the spirit we love. Those vows are about what we have, Daniel, and I want to follow that to the only place it can take us."

"Yeah?"

"If you try to deny it, I won't believe you." But she gave another little shiver of fear, because this was more naked than the state of her body, telling him that she knew more about the state of his heart than he would admit to himself.

He took hold of her and barged his forehead into her chest. They were pressed skin to skin, except for the roughness of the cutoff jeans against her thighs. "I do love you," he said. "I've wanted to say it for weeks. I've wanted to make you marry me—"

"You don't need to make me. I'd marry you in a heart-beat." She stroked his hair, inhaling the familiar fragrance of it, feeling the musky silk of it against her jaw.

"Yeah, and you'd regret it in five."

"No." She cupped his face in her hands and kissed him, little teasing, swooping movements that made him groan in frustration and chase her with his mouth.

"Prove it," he said. "*Promise* it. How do you know? Have you answered any of the real questions?"

"I want us to answer those together, the two of us, not on my own."

"You have to answer them on your own, first. Where would we live?"

"Here. I have the money to buy Paula and Jordan out."

"What would you do?"

"I told you about the job at Spring Ridge. The hours are way more flexible than I've had before. I want to keep working at Aaron's."

"What would your family say?"

"I don't care. I'm not going to let Dad put me in a strait-jacket, the way Kyle did. I'm not Kyle. More to the point,

I'm not Dad. We fought about it when he was up here. He doesn't understand yet, but I'm hoping one day he will."

"How do you know it won't turn ugly? We won't have this forever. The newness of it." But he was touching her as he spoke, brushing his fingers over her skin, because the newness, not even so new anymore, was irresistible.

"Do you think we only feel like this because it's new? It's not new. It's six years old."

"Big gap where it wasn't happening."

"Plenty of time for us to change. And we didn't. We stayed the same. Wanting this. Wanting everything."

"Shh," he said. "I can't—" He shook his head. "Hell, I just want to hold you."

"So *do* that."

He didn't need to be asked twice. They were both losing patience, losing control. She found the fastening of his jeans and slid the zipper down. It was tight, strained by the way he filled out the fabric with his need for her. He twisted around and lay back on the couch and she pulled his clothing down, fighting the hard cast all the way.

Then she straddled him again, as they lay half on their sides. So hard to wait, hard to get it right. It only made them hungrier. He held her hips and she moaned as he slid into her and it didn't last long after that because they were both too roiled up inside, both proving a point about sex and love and connection.

His body was hot and hard, and he could give her so much more than he seemed to know. Tenderness and humor and generosity and honor. Why the *hell* did he think those things weren't worth more than—well, than anything else she could ever imagine? Worth more than all Kyle's intellect and arguments, all Dad's arrogance about medicine and life.

Daniel, I love you and I hate what you're doing. Oh, Dan. Oh, I want this, and you're killing me with it.

She climaxed almost in anger, and sensed that he did, too.

Yes, I'll take this from you, but that doesn't mean I buy into what you think it means.

Afterward, she lay there breathless against him, while he shifted beneath her for the sake of his leg. "Happy now?" His voice was creaky and leaden.

"Not very."

"No… Well…" *Didn't I tell you,* his stiffly held body seemed to say.

There was just one thing wrong with Judy and Aaron's idea that she should walk away, and make him come after her. She didn't believe it was going to happen. He hadn't spoken one word to keep her here, or made one movement to stop her leaving. She knew he was going to let her go. She got dressed in silence, while he lay there with eyes closed.

This was one of those times—she'd known a few of them with Kyle—where she couldn't believe that this was really her and that this was really happening. She made all the right movements, but it was as if she'd left her own body and was watching it from above. These were her hands, reaching around to fasten her bra, but they didn't feel like hers. These were her feet, slipping into the gray shoes, but they were miles from the rest of her body.

She just had to gather the few things she had here and go back to Andy's and work from there. The first hour of the rest of her life.

Because Daniel wasn't going to stop her. He was hurting just as much as she was about it, but he was going to let it happen anyway. He didn't even need her to take care of him physically until he'd mastered the crutches, because he had Greg and Lena only a phone call away.

Daniel's cell phone rang just as she thought this, and she snatched it up, since it was out of his reach, half expecting that it would be Greg or Lena themselves on the line. But it wasn't, it was a stranger. "I'm calling about the cars." He'd seen the ad on the internet, he was interested in the possibility of Chevy parts, and he was only fifteen minutes away, could he come over?

"Let me put you on to the owner," she said, and brought the phone to Daniel.

He took it, and she left him talking to the potential parts buyer about what models he had and what condition they were in. She was grateful to the caller. He'd helped them avoid the last horrible moment. Eye contact. Or a shrug.

She thought she probably would see Daniel again, at some point. This wasn't the *very* end. Life was messier than that. There would be something. A piece of his clothing left at Andy's. Or just a need to say a halfway decent goodbye. If she took the position at Spring Ridge, they'd eventually run into each other, probably more than once.

But it was the end as far as anything that really mattered.

Chapter Seventeen

Daniel ended the call just seconds after Scarlett left the house. He felt gutted and paralyzed and wrong. The guy wanting Chevy parts would be here soon. He seemed keen to nail a deal before anyone else beat him to it, which was funny, really, when you considered that the parts had been sitting there for so long.

"How the hell am I going to show him around?" Daniel muttered to himself, registering the reality of wheelchair and crutches as his two options.

He picked the crutches. Surely they couldn't be that hard, and they had the advantage of being in reach.

But they were pretty damned annoying, and his leg hurt more than he wanted it to, dangling in the awkward cast. He gritted his teeth and refused to let it beat him. He heard Scarlett's car door slam, but then the engine didn't start. He didn't know why it wasn't starting, just knew he shouldn't need to listen out for her every move like this, when there was nothing left for them to do or say.

He fumbled and wrenched his way back into his clothing, then hopped and hobbled out to the deck. There were two Chevys of about the right vintage in a shed almost on the back boundary, and another couple at the far end of one of the rows that he'd left intact with the 'dozer because almost all the vehicles in it were worth more than scrap.

Scarlett's car was still here. He could just see it in the front yard, his vision encroached on by the corner of the house. She might not know he was out here. If she did, she probably wouldn't approve. As far as his convalescence went, he was attempting to run before he could walk.

Story of his life, if you wanted to look at it that way. Bold moves and setbacks, growing up and then coming back home, everything in the wrong order.

Just look at the damned junkyard of cars. How many different things had it been to him over the years? Father-son bond. Symbol of squandered ambition. Eyesore. Treasure chest. Trip wire. Even the new sense of hope he and Paula had about giving the money they earned from them to charity hadn't been a one-way street, because his accident with the 'dozer had been the result.

Maybe nothing ever was a one-way street.

Maybe all of it was a roller coaster instead.

Maybe this was just life.

Life in all its dirty, wonderful, complicated, precious, terrible glory.

What choice did you have?

What *choice?*

The question hit him like a brick, and powered the fight and the stubbornness back into him.

Dad, you *had choices and you didn't take them. And I'm your son, but I'm* not *you. Damn it, you had the choice to fight for what you wanted, and what was possible. You always* had *that. And you could never take it. You never fought. You never kept the end in view. You never saw what you wanted and made it happen.*

I'm different.

I'm not you.

Scarlett had said it, too, just now. *I'm not Dad.*

Snap. Something in common.

Scarlett still hadn't started her engine. She was just sitting there. He bumped his way farther around the deck so he could see what was happening and there was her silhouette behind the wheel, hands gripping, head bent forward, just the way she'd been that first day beside the highway when he hadn't known who she was.

She didn't know that he'd come out and was watching her.

His heart gave a sickening flip, and he just couldn't *stand* to see her hurting this bad. It didn't need to happen. For once in his life—no, for the rest of his life, if she really meant what she'd said to him—he was going to believe in hope and in the possibility of being different. He was going to see what he wanted and make it happen.

He bumped and hobbled down the steps, and she must have heard, or looked up and seen. He saw the car door open. She climbed out and looked at him, then came walking slowly forward, something dawning in her face but not dawning fast enough. She didn't know yet. She didn't dare to believe.

But he did, now. He dared to believe, and he needed her to know it.

He cleared his throat.

"I want to give it a shot," he said, and saw her face start to change, saw the sun begin to come out in her smile.

"Say that again?" She stopped. The witch, she was making him come to her, and to hell with the crutches.

Okay, then. You want it, Scarlett, you got it.

He hobbled closer. "I want to marry you and make it happen."

"Just like that?" Her voice shook a little. The setting sun shafted onto her hair. "Isn't this a little different to what you said about ten minutes ago?"

"So I've been thinking."

"You think fast."

"I think with my gut."

"I like that. I think I need to hear more about it."

"More than happy to oblige with that."

"Yeah?" Her smile went wider.

"I want to live with you and laugh with you and plan with you." He was smiling, too. Grinning. Crazy with happiness. "I want to go with my gut and forget everything else. I want to believe in this, and make it happen. I want to stay here, and make this land beautiful, and make plans with you, and be proud of you, and know you're proud of me."

"Oh, I am. I'm incredibly proud of you. I—I can't believe you're saying this. I didn't think you would. I—I was so scared you were just going to let me go, Daniel."

"Would have come for you eventually. Would have seen sense. Happened a bit sooner than it might have, when I looked at those cars."

"The cars?"

"Because it's all in how you look at them. It's up to you. Whether they're a depressing heap of junk or a world of possibility."

"A world of possibility..." she echoed on a whisper, as if she liked the idea. Loved it.

"I love you so much. Marry me, Scarlett. You don't know how many times I've wanted to say that. Just marry me." His voice cracked and the crutches were almost too much. He couldn't keep hobbling toward her. They had to meet each other halfway.

She seemed to know it. She watched him for a second or two, watched the shaky, unbalanced way he stood, and then surged forward, while he felt like he might burst with happiness and certainty and visions of the future.

She reached him and put her arms around him and brought her mouth close to his. "Yes, Daniel Porter," she said. "Just—yes!"

* * * * *

HEART & HOME

Heartwarming romances where love can
happen right when you least expect it.

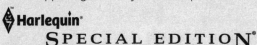

COMING NEXT MONTH
AVAILABLE MAY 29, 2012

#2191 FORTUNE'S PERFECT MATCH
The Fortunes of Texas: Whirlwind Romance
Allison Leigh

#2192 ONCE UPON A MATCHMAKER
Matchmaking Mamas
Marie Ferrarella

#2193 THE RANCHER'S HIRED FIANCÉE
Brighton Valley Babies
Judy Duarte

#2194 THE CAMDEN COWBOY
Northbridge Nuptials
Victoria Pade

#2195 AN OFFICER, A BABY AND A BRIDE
The Foster Brothers
Tracy Madison

#2196 NO ORDINARY JOE
Michelle Celmer

You can find more information on upcoming Harlequin® titles,
free excerpts and more at www.HarlequinInsideRomance.com.

HSECNM0512

REQUEST YOUR FREE BOOKS!
2 FREE NOVELS PLUS 2 FREE GIFTS!

◆ Harlequin®

SPECIAL EDITION

Life, Love & Family

YES! Please send me 2 FREE Harlequin® Special Edition novels and my 2 FREE gifts (gifts are worth about $10). After receiving them, if I don't wish to receive any more books, I can return the shipping statement marked "cancel." If I don't cancel, I will receive 6 brand-new novels every month and be billed just $4.49 per book in the U.S. or $5.24 per book in Canada. That's a saving of at least 14% off the cover price! It's quite a bargain! Shipping and handling is just 50¢ per book in the U.S. and 75¢ per book in Canada.* I understand that accepting the 2 free books and gifts places me under no obligation to buy anything. I can always return a shipment and cancel at any time. Even if I never buy another book, the two free books and gifts are mine to keep forever.

235/335 HDN FEGF

Name	(PLEASE PRINT)

Address	Apt. #

City	State/Prov.	Zip/Postal Code

Signature (if under 18, a parent or guardian must sign)

Mail to the **Reader Service**:
IN U.S.A.: P.O. Box 1867, Buffalo, NY 14240-1867
IN CANADA: P.O. Box 609, Fort Erie, Ontario L2A 5X3

Not valid for current subscribers to Harlequin Special Edition books.

Want to try two free books from another line?
Call 1-800-873-8635 or visit www.ReaderService.com.

* Terms and prices subject to change without notice. Prices do not include applicable taxes. Sales tax applicable in N.Y. Canadian residents will be charged applicable taxes. Offer not valid in Quebec. This offer is limited to one order per household. All orders subject to credit approval. Credit or debit balances in a customer's account(s) may be offset by any other outstanding balance owed by or to the customer. Please allow 4 to 6 weeks for delivery. Offer available while quantities last.

Your Privacy—The Reader Service is committed to protecting your privacy. Our Privacy Policy is available online at www.ReaderService.com or upon request from the Reader Service.

We make a portion of our mailing list available to reputable third parties that offer products we believe may interest you. If you prefer that we not exchange your name with third parties, or if you wish to clarify or modify your communication preferences, please visit us at www.ReaderService.com/consumerschoice or write to us at Reader Service Preference Service, P.O. Box 9062, Buffalo, NY 14269. Include your complete name and address.

SPECIAL EDITION

Life, Love and Family

USA TODAY bestselling author

Marie Ferrarella

enchants readers in

ONCE UPON A MATCHMAKER

Micah Muldare's aunt is worried that her nephew is going to wind up alone in his old age...but this matchmaking mama has just the thing! When Micah finds himself accused of theft, defense lawyer Tracy Ryan agrees to help him as a favor to his aunt, but soon finds herself drawn to more than just his case. Will Micah open up his heart and realize Tracy is his match?

Available June 2012

Saddle up with Harlequin® series books this summer and find a cowboy for every mood!

Available wherever books are sold.

www.Harlequin.com

HSE65674

*A grim discovery is about to change everything for
Detective Layne Sullivan—including how she
interacts with her boss!*

*Read on for an exciting excerpt of the upcoming book
UNRAVELING THE PAST by Beth Andrews….*

SOMETHING WAS UP—otherwise why would Chief Ross
Taylor summon her back out? As Detective Layne Sullivan
walked over, she grudgingly admitted he was doing well.
But that didn't change the fact that the Chief position
should have been hers.

Taylor turned as she approached. "Detective Sullivan,
we have a situation."

"What's the problem?"

He aimed his flashlight at the ground. The beam illumi-
nated a dirt-encrusted skull.

"Definitely a problem." And not something she'd expected. Not here. "How'd you see it?"

"Jess stumbled upon it looking for her phone."

Layne looked to where his niece huddled on a log. "I'll
contact the forensics lab."

"Already have a team on the way. I've also called in units
to search for the rest of the remains."

So he'd started the ball rolling. Then, she'd assume command while he took Jess home. "I have this under control."

Though it was late, he was clean shaven and neat, his flat
stomach a testament to his refusal to indulge in doughnuts.
His dark blond hair was clipped at the sides, the top long
enough to curl.

The female part of Layne admitted he was attractive.

The cop in her resented the hell out of him for it.

"You get a lot of missing-persons cases here?" he asked.

"People don't go missing from Mystic Point." Although plenty of them left. "But we have our share of crime."

"I'll take the lead on this one."

Bad enough he'd come to *her* town and taken the position she was meant to have, now he wanted to mess with *how* she did her job? "Why? I'm the only detective on third shift and your second in command."

"Careful, Detective, or you might overstep."

But she'd never played it safe.

"I don't think it's overstepping to clear the air. You have something against me?"

"I assign cases based on experience and expertise. You don't have to like how I do that, but if you need to question every decision, perhaps you'd be happier somewhere else."

"Are you threatening my job?"

He moved so close she could feel the warmth from his body. "I'm not threatening anything." His breath caressed her cheek. "I'm giving you the choice of what happens next."

What will Layne choose? Find out in
UNRAVELING THE PAST by Beth Andrews,
available June 2012 from Harlequin® Superromance®.

And be sure to look for the other two books
in Beth's THE TRUTH ABOUT THE SULLIVANS series
available in August and October 2012.

Harlequin *Romance*

A touching new duet from fan-favorite author

SUSAN MEIER

First Time DADS!

When millionaire CEO Max Montgomery spots
Kate Hunter-Montgomery—the wife he's never forgotten—
back in town with a daughter who looks just like him, he's
determined to win her back. But can this savvy business tycoon
convince Kate to trust him a second time with her heart?

Find out this June in

THE TYCOON'S SECRET DAUGHTER

And look for book 2 coming this August!

NANNY FOR THE MILLIONAIRE'S TWINS

Saddle up with Harlequin® series books this summer
and find a cowboy for every mood!

www.Harlequin.com

HRI7811

Get swept away with author

Carolyne Aarsen

Saving lives is what E.R. nurse Shannon Deacon excels at. It also distracts her from painful romantic memories and the fact that her ex-fiancé's brother, Dr. Ben Brouwer, just moved in next door. She doesn't want anything to do with him, but Ben is also hurting from a failed marriage…and two determined matchmakers think Ben and Shannon can help each other heal. Will they take a second chance at love?

Healing the Doctor's Heart

Home to
Hartley Creek

Available June 2012 wherever books are sold.